V V

A HORROR STORY FOR CHILDREN

RICHARD RIPPON

Cover by Lana Rippon

For Celia and Lana

CONTENTS

CHAPTER ONE

THE CALL

In the days that followed, we would think back to that phone call.

The three of us were in the kitchen – me, Lizzie, and Noah – just hanging out and annoying Mam with plans for Christmas, while she tried to make lunch. Lizzie was bouncing around the place, like she always does, asking if we could get the decorations down from the loft room.

"It's too early," replied Mam. "There's plenty of time for all of that."

"There's four houses in the street that have already got theirs up," said Lizzie, starting to whine. "We're always last."

That much was true. A man across the street had been stapling sheets of white felt and fairy lights to his roof just that morning. I'd watched him from my bedroom window for twenty minutes, wondering if he might fall off at some point. He hadn't.

"We'll do it soon," said Mam. I could tell she was getting frustrated, by the way she slapped the ham onto the bread. "But when we do, we might just need a bit of muscle, Noah."

She always liked to do this fake, flirty thing with him, just to wind me up. And he always joined in, of course. So he grinned really cheesily and flexed his arms like he was hench. His arms were actually looking quite a bit bigger, not that I cared.

"If you roll those eyes any further, Raine Russell, they'll roll out the back of your skull and down the road," she said.

"Why don't you ask Martin?" I said, "If you want muscles, I mean."

Noah sniggered. Mam raised her eyebrows and gave me a stern look, but when she turned to wash her hands in the sink, I could tell she was smiling too.

Martin always said that he just had a fast metabolism. He ate loads, but never seemed to put on any weight. Before he had to sell it to buy comics, he had ridden a scooter with a red helmet. Noah had called him 'The Matchstick Man'.

Lizzie just smiled awkwardly, and flicked back her long hair. She never liked when we made fun of Martin, but that's because she couldn't remember a time before him.

I remember Dad.

So we sat on the kitchen bench and ate our sandwiches. I watched Mam as she looked out through the kitchen window across the fields. Our house was built about a hundred years ago, at the end of a farmer's lane. Then they added a load of modern houses around us, so ours looks kind of old and shabby in comparison. Mam says we should be happy that we have a bit more originality and space, not like those 'little boxes'.

Luckily, they didn't build behind us, so our back garden just sort of runs out where the fields start. In the summer, it glowed with bright yellow rapeseed, but now in December, it was just dark-brown, churned-up dirt. Even so, I was jealous that Lizzie's room faced that way, and she could see Noah coming when he cycled along the tracks to and from our house.

Noah lived in an estate on the other side of the fields. When he clicked his bedroom light on and off, we could see it from Lizzie's bedroom, like a little flashing beacon on the horizon.

He shared a room with his older brother, who still hung around outside the high school, even though he officially left about four years ago. His sister had her own kid that lived with them too, so he was already an uncle. I think they had even less money than us. Their dad wasn't around either, but even so, it must have been pretty cramped in there, which was probably one of the reasons he was always at our house.

That and the fact he was my best friend.

Noah's mam was a nurse in the maternity ward when I was born, so they'd got to know each other a little bit. I should have come along three weeks later than I did, and Mam sometimes said I came out 'undercooked', like there was something wrong with me. But other times, when she was happier with me, she'd say that 'I couldn't wait to get into the world'.

Noah's mam stopped being a nurse at some point. My mam said it was to 'pursue other interests', but she never seemed to do much of anything, so who knows what those interests were meant to be. She also said Noah's mam was a 'funny woman', but she never seemed that funny to me whenever I saw her at the precinct, carrying her bags of shopping.

The dishwasher was broken, so I was helping to wash the dishes at the sink, when Martin breezed in and grabbed

3

her from behind, in a way that made me cringe. Mr Socks came in with him, meowing loudly until Lizzie gave in and got him a sachet of cat food, which he ate so quickly, it made the bell on his collar jingle.

"I wasn't expecting to see you back so soon," she said, kissing him with a cuteness that nearly made my lunch reappear.

"I locked up early," said Martin, as if it was some kind of treat for us all. We all knew it was because he didn't have any customers, just his geeky friends who didn't have anything better to do than hang out in the shop. I'm a kid, and I could have told you that a comic shop was never going to work in the precinct. People just go there for the off-licence, the bookies and the little supermarket.

Martin's shop has the worst name ever: *Wormhole Books*. I knew that it was meant to mean something far-out about space travel, but people just called it *Bumhole Books*, or said that it was a hole full of worms. Which is exactly what it was. Human worms.

Mam had given him the money to get started with the place, but it was a decision I think she regretted. On one side of the room was a mural of a generic superhero. In other words, it was one invented and painted badly by his friend, G. He was this overweight guy who was always at the shop and Martin sometimes went bowling with him. There were no radiators at Wormhole Books, so the only warmth came from a portable gas heater that made everything feel damp and caused mould to grow on the walls behind the wooden comic boxes. The smell of that, mixed with G's armpits was a real experience. Everyone thought the name 'G' sounded cool, but his real name was Gideon. *Gideon* for god's sake.

Anyway, it was about then, with Martin hugging Mam, and the rest of us feeling pretty awkward about it, that the phone rang. We would think back to that moment, because it was the last time anything felt vaguely normal. If we'd have known what was to follow, we might have clung onto that reality a little bit harder.

It was the landline that rang, which was strange in itself. A weak little warble that usually meant a nuisance call. Mam disentangled herself from Martin and lifted the phone from the cradle.

"Hello," she said. "Who? No, I think you've got the wrong…"

Noah slid off the worktop, caught my eye and nodded towards the door.

"I don't know anyone by that name, never mind a relative…" she went on.

Lizzie started to say something and I shushed her. She pursed her lips, like she always did when she was angry, but didn't want to say anything she'd regret.

"I'm sorry this person is unwell, but I really don't think I can help you," said Mam, looking up at the ceiling in exasperation.

Martin, who had started to make a sandwich of his own, stopped what he was doing to listen.

"Yes, well I'm sorry to hear that, but…"

I could tell she was getting annoyed, shifting her weight from one foot to the other, and putting her hand on her hip.

"Fine," she said, shaking her head. "Let me speak to him. He's obviously mistaken."

Martin was rolling up slices of ham into tubes and munching through them. He mouthed, 'just hang up', with a disgusting amount of meat hanging from his teeth.

Someone else was on the line. I could hear a different voice reverberating from the receiver, and although the words themselves were impossible to hear, the deep tone rattled the receiver and seemed to fill the room.

Mam's expression changed.

Her mouth dropped open, as if she'd just realised something of tremendous importance. Her eyes darted from side to side, as if she was taking in a lot of information at once. The rich timbre of the voice rumbled on for what felt like an eternity. Mam had started to nod her head, slowly and rhythmically, like one of those novelty dogs you might see in the back of an old car. A glob of spittle was in danger of falling from her bottom lip.

I looked at Lizzie and Noah, and they too were mesmerised by her trance-like state, as if it was infectious. Then suddenly, the noise from the receiver stopped.

"Yes," said Mam, her eyes now locked and unblinking. "We must get ready."

She extended the phone towards Martin without looking in his direction.

"Who is it?" he whispered, but she ignored him.

He took the phone and held it to his ear.

"Hello?" he said, raising his big furry caterpillar eyebrows.

The deep baritone began again. Martin suddenly straightened from his usual slouch, and stood to attention, dropping a slice of ham as he did so. Noah snorted a laugh, but Martin's expression was deadly serious.

"Yes," he said, flatly, eyes fixed on the same invisible point as Mam's. "Yes, of course. Yes."

Suddenly, the rumble on the phone stopped. After a moment, Martin carefully replaced the receiver, as if it was a precious and delicate artefact. He moved, so he was standing shoulder to shoulder with Mam. She looked at us, as if she had just realised we were in the room. Their faces broke into smiles at exactly the same time, not normal and friendly smiles, but exaggerated ones, as if they might split their mouths at the corners. I felt Lizzie grow tense beside me.

"Girls," said Mam, after a long, uncomfortable pause. "We're going to have a guest staying with us."

"Who?" I asked.

Grandma never left the home, even at Christmas, and although Martin had a family somewhere, he never talked about them, never mind having them over to stay.

"My Great Uncle Vivi," she said, smiling.

"Wait," said Lizzie. "Does that mean he's our Great Great Uncle?"

"Yes," said Mam, proudly.

"Why?" I asked. "I mean... I've never even heard of him."

"Uncle Vivi," she replied. "Has suffered a fall. He is unwell and he must be accommodated. He will arrive tonight."

There was something strange about her voice, as if she was reading a script from a television autocue. The fixed grin returned. I noticed there was a piece of spinach on one of her front teeth, but it didn't seem the right time to tell her.

"We must get ready," said Martin, robotically. "He must be accommodated."

"But where will he sleep?" I exclaimed. "I'm not sharing with Lizzie."

"I've got my school performance, Mam," she protested. "I need space."

Lizzie had been practising her dance routine every day for a week. We'd hear the thud-thud-thud of her cart-wheels in the sitting room below.

"We'll be too squashed, Mam," I added.

On the one occasion Grandma had stayed over, she'd

taken Lizzie's room, and me and Lizzie shared my bed. It had only been for a few nights, but it had been awful.

"In the loft room, I think," said Martin.

"Are you kidding?" I said, raising my voice a bit.

The loft room lay at the top of a short flight of rickety stairs from the landing, and had been the subject of many arguments. Lizzie had wanted the room to give her more space for cartwheeling, but I thought it was only right that I should have it, seeing I was the eldest. In the end, Martin had claimed it as his business office. *Ground Control*, he'd called it, and even though he'd put a desk up there, he hardly ever used it. It had become a dumping ground for things we never used, but weren't quite ready to get rid of.

Mam's smile dropped and she fixed me with a severe stare.

"In the loft room, I think," she said.

I looked down at the floor, and felt my face redden, embarrassed that all of this was happening in front of Noah.

"There's lots to be done," said Martin. The constant sarcasm had gone from his voice.

"Yes," said Mam, the smile returning. "Noah, I wonder if it might be a good idea if you headed home now, so the girls can help us prepare for our guest?"

"Oh," he said. I could tell he was surprised to be asked to leave. "Yes, I should probably go." He threw on his jacket and headed towards the back door, squeezing awkwardly past Mam and Martin. "I'll… er… I'll text you later, Raine," he said over his shoulder. Mr Socks, now with a full belly, darted past him, like a little black bullet with white feet. The door clicked shut and a moment later, I saw Noah cycle past the window and onto the track.

There was a heavy silence.

"There's lots to be done," said Martin.

8

VV

"Yes. Perhaps you girls could finish tidying up the kitchen, while we make a start upstairs?" said Mam.

"Yeah," I said, shrugging. "Whatever."

They stood and stared at us for an uncomfortably long time, before they filed out of the room. A moment later, I heard the creak of the loft stairs.

"What was all that about?" said Lizzie.

"I have no idea," I said.

We took our time washing the dishes, and putting food back in the fridge. Lizzie seemed to quickly forget the odd behaviour of the adults and started asking questions. How come we'd never heard of Great Uncle Vivi? Would he be staying for Christmas? Why was he poorly? Could he even die here in our house? All the time, I could hear the banging and clattering of Mam and Martin moving things around.

As soon as we were finished, I snuck upstairs as quietly as I could, with Lizzie following closely behind. When I tried to open my bedroom door, it was jammed with something. I squeezed myself into the room. It was Martin's desk, the one we were told was so important to have in the loft room. It had been dumped, without much thought, between the door and the bed.

I heard Lizzie, a little desolate cry from the next room.

I went to her. The room was full of cardboard boxes that I recognised immediately – the Christmas decorations. She stood among them, her eyes already welling up with tears.

"They've taken my bed," she said. She looked crestfallen. "I mean, I know Uncle Vivi is ill, and maybe he needs it more than me, but…"

"I'm sure Mam will have thought of something, Lizzie," I said, and put my hand on her shoulder. "I'll go and see what they're doing."

9

"Okay," she said, uncertainly.

I left her and crossed the landing to the loft room stairs. As I climbed the steps, each one creaked louder than the last. The stairs opened out into the room, with rickety bannisters at either side.

Mam was making the bed – Lizzie's bed – putting covers on the pillows. Behind her, Martin was frantically painting the room's single, circular window. Not the sill or the frame, but the glass itself. I watched as he loaded his brush with black gloss and daubed more on.

The step beneath me creaked and their eyes flicked in my direction.

"Sorry," I said. "What are you doing?"

Mam's mouth smiled, but her eyes didn't.

"We're getting ready for Uncle Vivi," she said.

"There's lots…"

"To be done," I said. "Yeah, I know. It's just, you've taken Lizzie's bed, without even saying anything to her. She's a bit upset."

Mam's stare intensified, as if she was trying to cut me in half with eyeball lasers. My neck felt hot, and my face reddened again.

"Uncle Vivi is our guest," she said. "We must *accommodate* him."

She looked at me in such a threatening way, that I almost gave up and went back to Lizzie. Instead I looked over her shoulder.

"Why are you painting the glass like that?" I asked.

Martin seemed to struggle to find any words. His bottom lip trembled slightly, but Mam answered for him.

"Uncle Vivi has a rare skin complaint, which means he cannot bear too much light."

Then she turned and strode into the shadows of the room, and when she returned, she was pushing something on casters that rattled on the wooden floor. Her face came into the light, and I could see that her forehead gleamed with sweat.

"There," she said.

It was a camp bed, with a stained, flimsy mattress.

She turned away from me abruptly and started putting a cover onto the duvet. Martin continued to slap more paint on the glass.

I opened my mouth to say something, to ask her why she was being so horrible, but I thought the better of it and started to drag the camp bed down to Lizzie's room.

When she saw it, her face dropped.

"Really?" she said.

"Let's just make some space for it," I said.

I helped her pile up the boxes at one side of the bedroom, and together we made up the camp bed with fresh sheets, and laid her quilt on top.

"I suppose it'll be okay," she said, more positively. "I'll just pretend to be camping for a couple of nights."

"It won't be for long," I said, ruffling her hair. "Anyway, you should see my room."

Mam and Martin showed no signs of stopping for tea, so I raided some crackers and cheese from the kitchen, and we ate them as we looked across the fields from Lizzie's bedroom window.

"Will Noah be in, do you think?" she said.

"I don't know. I'll text him."

I tapped him a message on my phone's cracked screen, and he answered almost immediately.

Noah: sup?

Raine: Nothing much. The olds are being well weird.

11

Noah:has uncle valerie showed up?

Raine:Lol. Nope. You in your room?

Noah:yep

Raine:Do it.

Noah:do what?

Raine:You know.

I scanned the numerous lights lining the horizon.

"Look, Lizzie," I said.

One of the lights flickered on and off a few times. She smiled. It was good to know Noah was there, across the sea of dirt and hedgerows, but even though he was so close, he felt so terribly far away at that moment. I hadn't wanted him to leave that afternoon.

Something felt very wrong.

CHAPTER TWO

THE ARRIVAL

The mysterious Uncle Vivi arrived later that night.

We were all watching TV, with Lizzie in charge of the remote, to make up for the camp bed incident. I think the power had gone to her head, and she was randomly flicking between the channels every few seconds. This kind of behaviour wouldn't usually have gone down well with Mam or Martin, but they both just watched in silence.

They had both changed their clothes. Mam was wearing a dress that was pretty, but far too light and summery for December. Martin had a short-sleeved shirt buttoned right up at the neck, and blue corduroy trousers, looking far smarter than he usually did, even though his hands were still stained with black paint. I was looking at the TV reflected in his black-rimmed glasses when the doorbell rang.

The adults rose from their seats together, like synchronised swimmers rising from a pool, and walked out of the room. Lizzie clicked off the TV and fastened her dressing gown. We followed them into the hallway. Martin opened the door, letting in a blast of icy air, and I stood on my tip-toes, trying to see over their shoulders.

There was a quick exchange of words that I couldn't quite make out, and a flurry of activity. Mam and Martin stepped to one side, and two burly, green-clad paramedics marched in carrying a gurney. They walked straight up the stairs, as if it weighed nothing at all. As they passed, I tried to see the man they were carrying, but his face was covered by an oxygen mask. All I saw was a shock of wispy black hair on the white pillow and bandages criss-crossed over his chest. I looked at Lizzie, whose eyes were wide with wonder, as if Santa himself had entered the house. A moment later, I heard the men huffing and puffing, and I imagined them negotiating the narrow steps to the loft.

"Oh yes," I heard my mother say, and I realised someone else was at the front door. "Do come in."

A severe-looking woman stepped inside. She was quite a bit older than Mam, with tiny eyes and a puckered mouth that looked like she'd chewed on one too many lemons. She wore a tweed overcoat with a fancy green broach on the lapel and a paisley scarf over her hair.

She scanned our hallway with a critical eye, and looked wholly unimpressed.

"I must inspect Mister Virandi's accommodation," she said with a shrill voice.

"Stay down here, children," said Mam, and they all stomped up the stairs together.

The woman looked down on us as she climbed.

"Shut the door, Raine. It's freezing," said Lizzie.

I shushed her, and tried to hear what they might be saying at the top of the house.

Suddenly, the paramedics reappeared. They trouped downstairs with the empty gurney and left without saying a word. A moment later, we heard an engine start up, and as they turned in the cul-de-sac, the headlights swept through across the hall wall and they were gone.

I heard the creaking of the loft stairs.

"Lizzie," I said. "Come here."

I pulled her into the semi-darkness of the sitting room and left the door slightly ajar, so we could look out into the hallway. Mam, Martin and the strange woman appeared once more.

"That window is completely unacceptable," the woman was saying. "As you are aware, Mister Virandi has a highly acute sensitivity to light."

"We understand," said Mam. She had raised her chin defiantly, despite the fact that the woman was quite a bit shorter than her.

"The children could break the glass," the woman went on. "Or a pigeon could hit it from outside… An accident…"

"My children don't break windows," said Mam.

I felt proud of her for sticking up for us, despite the day's weirdness.

"We have it in hand," said Martin, as assertively as he could.

The woman sighed.

"I have been overseeing Mister Virandi's wellbeing for some time now," she said, her voice climbing even higher. "I think you need to make further allowances, and accommodate me in your home, so I can continue."

"No," said Mam firmly. "We will take care of everything."

I felt a sense of relief. There was no way I wanted that horrible woman in the house.

"Then I must be permitted access to him on a daily basis," she said indignantly. "Not only to ensure his recovery, but to consult with him about his business affairs. Something for which I am uniquely qualified.'

"That's fine," said Mam, opening the door for the woman. "But you have no cause for concern. We have him now."

The woman looked very put out and scowled at Mam and Martin. Before she turned to leave, she cast her eyes in our direction, although I felt sure she couldn't have been able to see us, I pulled Lizzie a step backward and I felt her body tense against mine.

The lady stepped out of the front door, and without a further word, Mam closed it behind her.

They turned towards us.

Lizzie and I jumped onto the settee and tried to look as innocent as possible. Mam and Martin walked in a moment later and sat on the armchairs.

"Who was that lady, Mam?" asked Lizzie.

"That was Mrs Krenwinkel," she replied.

"Kren*winkel*?" said Lizzie, suppressing a giggle.

"She wasn't very nice," I added.

Mam smiled. At first I thought she'd found some humour in Mrs Krenwinkel's name too, but then I realised she'd gone into fixed-grin mode again.

"That may be the case, but she's Uncle Vivi's assistant, and we must get along with her."

Martin leaned forward in his chair.

"I think we need to establish a few ground rules, girls," he said in his I'm-calling-the-shots voice. I tried to keep a straight face,

"This is a serious matter," said Mam, her eyes fixed and penetrating.

"You must not disturb Uncle Vivi," said Martin. "Under any circumstances."

"You must be quiet during the day," chipped in Mam. "No TV, no music, no internet and no video games."

"You must be in bed by eight-thirty every night," said Martin.

"You must do as you're told," said Mam. "The first time, every time."

There was a long, uncomfortable silence while they just looked at us.

"Are you serious?" I said.

Mam's answer was in her eyes.

"Oh, can't we meet him?" said Lizzie. "I mean, make get-well-soon cards and go up to visit him? He'll get so bored up there by himself."

"No," they said in unison.

"Not right now, Lizzie," said Mam, with a semblance of affection creeping back into her voice.

"Okay," she said, looking crestfallen and playing with the hem of her nightie.

"Well," said Martin, turning his head slowly, like an owl might. "Would you look at the time?" The clock on the wall said quarter to nine. "I think it's time you both went to bed."

"Now," added Mam, firmly.

"This is rubbish," I said. "It's the weekend. Come on, Lizzie."

Mam fixed me with a glare.

I left the room quickly. She had never hit me before, but I felt I might have been getting close. On the landing, we both stopped, looked up the loft stairs and listened in silence. We could hear nothing from above.

"Poor Uncle Vivi," whispered Lizzie.

"Come into my room," I said, and took her hand. "Just for a minute." We squeezed past Martin's desk and sat on the bed. "Don't you think they're being totally weird?" I said in a low voice.

The room was dark, but Lizzie's face glowed a warm orange from the streetlight outside. I could see her wrestle with the question. She so rarely had a bad word to say about anyone, never mind members of her own family.

"I think they're just nervous about him," she said. "It looks like he's really ill."

"Who is he anyway?" I said. "Have you ever heard Mam talking about him? I haven't. Not once."

"But she wouldn't let just anyone in," she said. "She must remember him. Maybe from when she was little?"

"It's like she's in a trance or something," I said. "And she's never usually this grumpy."

Lizzie bit her lip and shrugged.

She was smart and observant for a nine-year-old, but she had a big blind spot when it came to Mam and Martin.

We sat quietly together for a moment, listening. There was no sound from the room above, and from the lounge below, only the endless chatter of the TV.

We hugged, in a bedroom routine that Mam had drummed into us. Then, with her unruly hair on my shoulder, I kissed the top of her head.

"Don't worry," she said, looking up at me, a smile breaking out on her face. "It's nearly Christmas."

"Night night, Lizzie."

She left the room, and soon after, I heard the creaks of the camp bed as she settled down upon it.

As I lay back on my own bed, and tried to sleep, a feeling of tremendous unease fell over me. It was like that daunting sense of dread on a Sunday night before school the next morning. I thought of the bandaged stranger above us, and Mam's and Martin's increasingly strange behaviour.

It took a while, but eventually my thoughts began to slip away from me, to be replaced by an awful dream.

People were hiding outside our house. They were gathered behind the hedges and fences of the cul-de-sac, waiting for an opportunity to get in. They looked as if they had been normal at some point, but something had happened and turned them savage. Their clothes were dirty and ragged, as if they'd been living in the fields for weeks, and their faces were gaunt with hunger.

And as I shone my torch between them, I could see they all had the same look in their eyes, something between desperation and determination. It was as if they craved something, but were not quite sure what.

It reminded me of the distant look of some of the old people at the nursing home where Mam worked. From behind, a hand roughly grabbed my shoulder, but before I could turn, I awoke with my heart beating hard and fast against my chest. I had to click on my bedside lamp to satisfy myself that I was still in my bedroom.

Everything was as it should be, apart from Martin's massive desk – the posters, the shelf of novels and the wardrobe with the missing door – but even then, something felt wrong, as if the world had somehow tilted.

CHAPTER THREE

THE RULES

B y the time I made it downstairs, Lizzie was already sitting at the kitchen table, with a bowl of cereal and a glass of milk.

She looked as tired as I felt, and gave me a half-hearted smile. She stared at something behind me, until I was forced to look. Mam's framed picture of a bright green forest had been taken down, and in its place, something had been written on the wall with marker pen:

1. No noise.
2. Bed at 8.30pm.
3. Do as you're told.
4. Do not go into the loft.

I read it and reread it.

It was written directly onto the paintwork in Mam's handwriting. The same Mam who told us off for putting our hands on the wall when we ran upstairs, and complained if the skirting boards got scuffed when we kicked our trainers off at the front door.

"What the hell?" I said to myself.

Martin appeared, striding in from the garage. He was wearing overalls that were heavily stained with paint and plaster. He ignored us completely and took a sharp turn into the hallway.

Lizzie looked at me, as I rolled my eyes and took a seat beside her. We could hear Mam and Martin's conversation in the lounge.

"I've checked the garage," said Martin, with an unfamiliar urgency. "We haven't got the right stuff."

"You'll have to go to the hardware store," said Mam.

"Can't you go?" replied Martin.

"I won't know what to get," she replied, tersely.

"I can give you a list," he said, raising his voice slightly.

"That's no good," said Mam. "We need to get this right."

"Well, you'd better drive me," snapped Martin. "I can't carry everything we need."

"But what about…"

There was some whispering, but it was drowned out by Lizzie's spoon clinking against the bowl.

There was a pause and Mam marched into the kitchen. She looked oddly dishevelled, as if she hadn't had the chance to get ready properly. Her hair was frizzy at the sides, but her fringe lay flat against her head, and it reminded me of the time we went camping. She was wearing her scruffy work clothes. Not the leggings and t-shirt she might put on to push the vacuum around, but the ripped jeans and grubby sweatshirt.

"We need to pop out," she said. "To get a few things."

Her eyes darted from mine to Lizzie's and back again. If we'd thought she was acting uptight the previous day, she seemed to be on another level.

"Okay," I said, to fill the uncomfortable silence that followed.

"You know the rules," she said. "As you can see, I've written them here, so no one can say they forgot them." She pointed to the list. "Under no circumstances must you disturb Uncle Vivi."

"Okay, Mam," said Lizzie, in a very quiet voice. She sounded scared and I didn't like it.

"We were planning to go into town with Noah anyway," I said. "Right, Lizzie?"

This was partly true, but Lizzie hadn't been invited until that moment. She raised her eyebrows a little, but caught on quickly.

"Yeah," she said, brightly. "Some early Christmas shopping."

Mam's eyes continued to jump between us, as if she was calculating the risk, working out how much she could trust us.

"Alright then," she said, just as Martin reappeared and stood at her side. "That might be for the best."

She pointed to the rules again and looked at us ominously before leaving the room. Moments later, I heard the door slam shut and Mam's rusty old Corsa sputter to life.

I poured myself a bowl of cereal, added milk, and a generous sprinkling of sugar.

"You okay?" I asked.

She pulled a face.

"Weird dreams," she said.

"Me too," I replied. "Let's just get out of here for a while."

She nodded.

As if on cue, Noah's face appeared at the kitchen window. He put his mouth on the glass and blew, so his cheeks puffed out and his mouth looked like a huge, pink cave you could almost walk into.

"You mean you haven't even seen him?" he said, once he'd stepped inside.

He wasn't wearing a jacket, and his hoodie was soaked with rain. It had a brown streak on the back where mud had sprayed up from the back wheel of his bike.

"Not really," I said.

Noah had a habit of paying exactly zero attention to the weather when he dressed. On a hot summer day, you could see him at the precinct in a massive puffer jacket, but then he could roll up in the snow wearing a sleeveless t-shirt and a beanie hat.

"Well, we saw him when they took him upstairs, but that's about it," I said.

"He looked pretty messed up," chimed Lizzie.

"Really?" said Noah, with an interest that instantly made me feel nervous.

"No, not really," I said. "He had a bandage on his chest, that's all. Like I said, they whipped him upstairs so fast, we didn't get a proper look."

"Wouldn't you like to?" he said.

"What?"

"Get a good look at him?" he said, eyes widening with a familiar look of mischief.

I pointed to the rules with my spoon.

"Oh wow," he said, taking a while to read them. As he did, I noticed a bruise on his temple that hadn't been there the day before. Could that have been his brother? One of his mam's friends? He seemed to notice me staring, so I looked down. "She's taking this very seriously."

"She is," I said. "They are."

Between mouthfuls of cereal, I filled him in on the weirdness that had taken over the house, including the unpleasant Mrs Krenwinkel. He listened carefully, while helping himself to a bowl, and Lizzie chipped in details of her own that I might have otherwise missed.

"So, do you always do what you're told?" he asked when we'd finished.

"No, but…"

"Then let's sneak upstairs. Take a peak." He smiled and a rivulet of milk dribbled down his brown chin. "If he's as banged-up as you say he is, he's not going to notice. He'll probably be asleep. You know… medicated."

"I don't care. I think it's a bad idea," I said, taking my bowl to the sink and rinsing it under the tap.

"No one would ever know," he said, raising his eyebrows and shaking his head.

"I'd quite like to see him," said Lizzie.

"There you go," said Noah. "We'll all have a look at Uncle Vanessa…"

"Vivian," giggled Lizzie.

"Whatever. Then we'll go straight into town. Alright everyone?"

"No… wait," I said.

It was too late.

They had already abandoned the table. I followed them into the hallway, Noah towering at the front, a good foot and a half taller than Lizzie, who ran behind him. He took the steps two at a time. Lizzie pulled herself up on the bannister as she went, as if trying to make herself sound lighter on the stairs.

"This is wrong," I mouthed, when we'd assembled on the landing.

He held an index finger to his lips and whispered a shush.

We looked up the steps to the loft.

"Well?" I whispered.

Noah looked down at me, and I could see the devilment had left his eyes, replaced by what? Apprehension?

"He's your uncle," he whispered. "Don't you think you should go first?"

He stepped back.

"Are you kidding?" I said. "We're here now, you wuss. Come on Lizzie."

I took her hand and started up the stairs. The first step creaked terribly.

"Raine," said Lizzie, trying hard to keep her voice low while she pulled me back. "Wait, I know where to stand." She squeezed past me and put her foot on the outermost edge of the step. It took her weight without a sound. "Stand where I stand."

She stood right in the middle of the next step and it gave no more than a tiny groan. I followed her path exactly. Behind me, I could sense Noah moving as quietly as his lanky frame would allow.

At the top, the floor gave a low creak, as if it was giving us a final warning. Lizzie edged further into the room, while Noah lurched behind. His breath on the back of my neck made me shiver, which was part nervousness and part something else altogether.

The room was dark, but there was still some light from the circular window. Martin had abandoned the paint job after only a few coats, and there were still light patches where it did not completely block the daylight outside.

Lizzie's bed stood in the middle of the room, with several feet between it and the walls. I could see little felt stickers – stars, planets and comets – that she'd put on the headboard years previously. To the side was a metal intravenous stand with four full bags of blood hanging from it.

The man in the bed looked ancient. He was balding, with a few wisps of jet-black hair struggling to cover a pale, flaking scalp. He looked terribly thin, like the poor people I'd seen on a YouTube video about World War II. His eyes were closed, and seemed to have sunk into his head much deeper than should have been possible, and his skull was covered in the thinnest layer of skin, with heavy lines around the corners of his mouth.

There were several pillows behind him, elevating his head and shoulders from the bed. The blankets covered him to his waist and his curled hands lay upon them, the fingers like the long, wizened talons of a dead bird.

His torso had been dressed with clean white bandages that crossed over the heart. His chest seemed to have collapsed in on itself, but managed to rise and fall with each shallow breath.

Lizzie nudged me with her elbow and pointed. Against the wall was a battered old leather suitcase. It was scuffed at every edge, and tied to the handle was an address label. On the lid, there was a faded monogram:

V V

There was a strange, musty odour in the room that hadn't been there before. I was used to the smell of old people, from helping Mam at the care home, but this was different. This wasn't down to old-fashioned soap or talc, or not washing properly. This was a bad smell, the smell of dirt and rot and doom. It had an otherness, a *wrongness*. It was something that didn't belong. Not here at least.

"What's that?" whispered Lizzie, curling up her nose when the stench reached her.

Suddenly, the old man's eyes flicked open, and we all jumped backwards.

The irises of had a pale blue luminescence, and it felt as though someone had switched on a light.

Lizzie instinctively grabbed me in fright, and I realised I was holding Noah's arm.

We were transfixed by his stare. He didn't seem surprised to see us. It was as if he'd been aware of us all along, and only just decided to let us know about it.

"Children," he said, with a tone which could have been a greeting or a statement, it was hard to tell. His voice was as piercing as his eyes, and deeper than could have been expected from his tiny, shrivelled frame.

"Hello," I said nervously.

Then there was a loud noise – one of Noah's size tens clunking down on the step behind him. Later, he would say that Lizzie and I were leaning so hard against him, he'd had to take a step back. We jostled against each other back down the stairs to the landing.

We looked at each other, eyes wide with fright, until Noah started to grin, and we all broke down into fits of silent giggles, holding on to each other for support.

CHAPTER FOUR

KRENWINKEL

Twenty minutes later, we were still shaking with exhilaration. Or maybe it was just the cold. It had been drizzling most of the morning, the kind of rain that soaked you instantly, and froze you to the bone.

The bus seemed to take forever to arrive, and when it did, we ran upstairs and huddled in the back seats, until our fingers and toes began to feel warm again. Lizzie sat next to me, and was quiet for a change. She was the kind of person who always liked to fill any dead air with chatter, so when she didn't, it got me worried. I think she was still processing our freaky introduction to Uncle Vivien.

Noah drew pictures in the window condensation. Sometimes, it was hard to believe he was almost two years older than me. He'd missed so much school, they'd made him drop back a year into my class. It wasn't all his fault. Not entirely. You could put some of it down to his dad leaving the way he did. He only ever told me bits about it, but you could piece them together without too much trouble.

Mr Nelson was a postman, and I think Noah got on

alright with him, when he was around anyway. He'd been a regular at *The Beehive* in the precinct, a pub that Mam always said was 'full of characters'. You'd always see him in the little outdoor smoking hut after he knocked off work, still in his blue uniform, puffing on skinny roll-up cigarettes as if his life depended on it. He'd always stay until closing time.

But it was in the pub that he met someone else. A woman. One morning, he'd left a letter on the mantelpiece, went off to work and never returned. They hadn't seen him since. It was something we had in common, Noah and me, but at least I knew where mine was. Not that it did any of us any good.

Mr Nelson's disappearance coincided with Noah's sister falling pregnant, and it was all too much for Noah's mam. I think she was quite a fragile person to begin with, but some awful switch seemed to have flicked in her mind, and now all she seemed to do was waddle to and from the shops. Mam said her bags were always clinking, which was her none-too-subtle way of saying she probably had a drinking problem.

The way I saw it, everyone in Noah's house pretty much looked out for themselves, even his sister's kid, who me and Lizzie once found wandering about on the grass verge near the chip shop, and had to take home. When Mrs Nelson answered the door, she just took her back in and closed the door, without even saying thanks.

Noah didn't like to talk about his dad much, and I was fine with that, because it usually led to a conversation about mine.

My dad had a job that was something to do with making sure factories did whatever they were supposed to be doing. It meant travelling around the country and some-times staying over in different places. Wherever he went, he'd bring me back a snow globe. I used to really like them when I was little. I can remember shaking them up, watching the glitter fall and imagining I lived in one of the little water-logged houses within. I can remember how he used to throw me up on his shoulders whenever we went for walks in the summer, and the smell of his aftershave. They still make it. It comes in a green barrel-shaped bottle, and sometimes I spray some in the chemist, just so I can remember him better.

One day there was a knock at the door – someone from his work, the boss in fact. Dad had been inspecting a roof at a factory, leant on a skylight that wasn't secure, and fallen thirty feet onto a potato waffle production line. Lizzie and I were too young for the funeral, but I can remember people coming to the house for sandwiches, and the smell of whisky and flowers in the lounge.

Sometime later, when I was messing around in the garage, I found a boxful of snowglobes, and realised that the ones that were fading on my windowsill probably hadn't come from wherever Dad said they had. As Mam said, it was probably difficult to find a snow globe anywhere near a pizza factory in Cleethorpes, and he wouldn't have wanted to disappoint me.

I still give the ones on my windowsill a shake sometimes.

Mam was really unhappy for a long time, then Martin came along and he made her laugh, which I suppose counts for something. I suppose it counts for a lot.

I THINK I'd blanked out for a while on the bus, because Noah waved his hands in front of my eyes to get my attention.

"Children," he said in a creepy voice, mimicking Uncle Vivi.

Lizzie giggled.

"You've been quiet," I said.

"Yes, well," she said. "I've been thinking."

I rolled my eyes, for Noah's benefit more than anything else.

He smiled.

"What about?" I asked.

"He *could* be our relative," she said. "Don't you think he looks a bit like mam? Across the eyes?"

"Nobody's eyes look like that, Lizzie," said Noah.

"Yeah, I know they're a mad colour, but can't you see the… what's the word?"

"The resemblance?" I suggested.

"That's it," said Lizzie. "Do you see it, Raine? The resemblance?"

"Yeah, maybe," I said.

The truth was, they did have a similar look, not just across the eyes, but their noses were the same – straight and thin.

"I just mean that maybe he is a relative," said Lizzie, raising her eyebrows, like she often did when she was trying to make a point and felt no-one was taking her seriously. "Just because we've never heard of him…"

"And he's incredibly weird…" interjected Noah.

"…doesn't mean he's not our real uncle and doesn't need our help," said Lizzie, her voice rising in pitch.

"Okay, Lizzie," I said. "You might be right. Mam's the one to ask, and she's in no mood for it at the minute. I just wish we hadn't gone up to the loft."

"Do you think he'll tell Mam that we did?" said Lizzie.

"I don't know," I said. "Maybe he's still so out of it, he'll not even remember."

"I think Mam would explode if he did," said Lizzie. "She's so uptight."

"Maybe he's loaded?" said Noah, and he held up a hand, rubbing his thumb and forefinger together. "Maybe that's why they're running around after him so much."

Lizzie looked confused. I could tell what she was thinking – *why would that make a difference?*

Either way, it kept us all thinking until the bus pulled into the station.

* * *

A SPARKLING NET of lights stretched out across the street against a sky of stubborn concrete grey, and their warm glow reflected back from the wet pavement beneath. In our part of the country, the sun didn't bother to rise much in winter. It just skirted over the horizon for a few hours before sneaking off and leaving a long, cold night behind it.

The security guard at the entrance to the shop gave Noah a look that let him know he was still remembered. There was a montage of photos at the top of the mall, featuring all the people they'd caught shoplifting. Noah was near the bottom, a really bad picture, taken when he'd had his old haircut. His hair was better now, and so was his behaviour. I sometimes thought these two things were linked. The guard gave Noah a respectful nod as we passed, but from the corner of my eye, I saw him whisper something into his walkie-talkie.

It was one of those shops where everything was very clean and organised, with all the clothes arranged neatly on old wooden tables. Impossibly beautiful people stared down at us from posters on the walls, as if they could see the holes in my socks through my wet trainers, or knew that my jacket was a lucky find at the British Heart Foundation. Those places always made me feel uncomfortable, and I felt too hot, a bead of sweat rolling uncomfortably from my neck down to the small of my back.

"What do you think of this, Raine?" said Lizzie.

She held up a camel-coloured jumper. It was beautiful and soft to the touch. I teased the price tag out of the sleeve and took a look. My eyebrows raised and Lizzie's face fell.

"For Helen?" said Noah. "Nice."

"It's lovely, Lizzie, but I don't think we can afford it, even if we pooled all our money together."

"But I've got some of my birthday money left," she said.

"I know, and I've got a little bit too, but not this much," I said as Lizzie tried to fold it back up, so it matched the others in the pile. "Maybe we could find something like it, but a bit cheaper?"

"Okay," she said.

She smiled meekly and looked at the floor.

I put a hand on her shoulder, but she shook it off and went to look at the t-shirts.

"I'm going to look at the men's stuff," said Noah, who seemed to have been oblivious to this little incident, and he wandered off towards the escalator.

Lizzie and I browsed aimlessly until we got bored, and went across the road to the department store, where we bought Martin some chocolate raisins and a four-pack of socks. We get him the same thing every year.

When we met up with Noah at the food place, I spotted a suspicious-looking bulge under his top, which he was trying his best to hide. Lizzie didn't notice, but I clocked it straight away. I gave him a look that told him I knew what he'd been up to, and he had to look away. I left it at that, and then we shared some chips which Noah drowned in too much mayonnaise.

* * *

By the time we got on the bus, it was getting dark.

I used the sleeve of my jacket to clear a rectangle of condensation from the window, so we could see where we were. We'd passed the precinct, the pub and the old barn, and we were driving alongside the dry stone wall that boarded the fields.

That's when I saw her.

My heart seemed to flip in my chest.

Instinctively, I grabbed onto Lizzie's forearm.

"Look," I said. "Look out there."

Lizzie moved closer to the window.

"What is it?" she said.

"Krenwinkel," I said, and the sound of her name inexplicably filled me with dread.

She was standing in the field, several feet behind the wall, unmistakable in her tweed suit and headscarf. A grey haze of rain fell down upon her, but she just stood and looked out from the field, as if she was patiently waiting for someone, or something. If she'd seen us on the top deck, or was even aware of the bus passing, she certainly didn't show it.

"What's she doing?" said Noah, wiping at his window, so he could see too.

"I have no idea," I said.

The bus took us past a patch of trees and she was gone from view.

The bizarre sighting of Mrs Krenwinkel had distracted us so much that Noah almost missed his stop. He ran down the bus, cradling whatever was under his hoodie, and almost flew down the stairs.

"It's so cold," said Lizzie, once the bus had got going again. "Why was she just standing there?"

I shrugged.

I didn't know, and the fact that I didn't know worried me more than I wanted to say.

BACK HOME, I peaked around the lounge door.

Mam and Martin sat together on the settee, silently watching a shopping channel. Their postures were identical – straight backs, hands on knees. Their faces were blank and expressionless.

Lizzie told me that she wanted a shower to warm up, so when she went upstairs, I went to the kitchen and hung our coats over the radiator to dry. Just as I turned to leave, I heard Mr Socks' cat flap rattle open. I looked down, expecting to see his little face, but instead I saw a human arm extend into the room holding something.

I had to stifle a scream, until I realised it was Noah. He dropped the plastic bag he was holding and pulled his arm back through the flap. He appeared at the window a moment later, smiling and holding out the palms of his hands, as if to say, *well what can you do?*

He winked, hopped onto his bike and set off down the track.

I picked up the bag and looked inside.

It was the expensive jumper Lizzie had found in the posh shop.

I pulled it out and held it to my face, revelling in the softness for a moment, while I looked out at the lights on the edge of the field beyond.

CHAPTER FIVE

THE SUITCASE

I decided to tell Lizzie about the jumper some other time and hid it at the back of my drawers. It couldn't have been much later that the doorbell rang, because Lizzie was still in the shower. I hid at the top of the stairs and witnessed one of the strangest conversations of my life.

Mam and Martin appeared side by side in the hallway, as if someone had sewn them together at the hip. Martin opened the door, and I could see Mrs Krenwinkel standing outside.

Her eye make-up had ran down her face and it looked as though she was wearing some kind of bizarre Halloween mask. She was shivering violently, but neither Mam nor Martin said a word, invited her in, or made a move to help her. Mam was usually the type to ask anyone in. Charity collectors, political canvassers, axe murderers – anyone. Usually, I would have expected her to usher her through, turn up the heating and say things like, 'you'll catch your death'.

Instead, it was Mrs Krenwinkel who spoke first:

"We are at the agreed hour, are we not." It didn't sound like a question.

Mam slowly looked at her watch, before moving to one side to let her in. Krenwinkel stepped inside, and I could see that her shoes were caked in thick mud from the field. She made no effort to wipe them on the mat, but Mam said nothing.

"How is Mr Virandi? Has he asked for me?" she said, looking up the stairs. Although I was confident she could not see me, I still ducked back behind the spindles of the staircase.

"No, he hasn't," said Mam, closing the door.

"It is getting dark. He will arise soon," she said, sounding exasperated. "He must be accommodated. I... *we* must attend to his needs."

"His needs are being well attended to, Mrs Krenwinkel," said Mam. "By those who can tend to them best."

Krenwinkel's brow furrowed.

"We'll see about that," she said.

She stepped off the mat, staring at Mam defiantly as she did so, and moved towards the stairs, leaving two large brown streaks on the floor. Mam threw her arm out and grabbed the newel post to block her path.

"Have your time while it lasts," she said icily. "He has no need for you now."

The two glared at each other a moment longer, until suddenly Mam spat in Krenwinkel's face. I was so shocked, I was afraid my sharp intake of breath might have been heard by one of them. Krenwinkel recoiled and wiped her face with her sleeve, then turned and walked stiffly up the stairs. I quickly ducked into the darkness of Lizzie's room and watched her as she continued from the landing to the loft.

Just then, Lizzie opened the bathroom door, releasing a

billow of steam with her. She'd wrapped herself in a large green towel, with a smaller one on her head, like a turban. I put a finger to my lips and she tiptoed into her room. We closed the door as much as we could while still being able to peek out.

A soft light spilled down from the loft onto the steps, and although we couldn't see them, or make out exactly what they were saying, we could hear their tone.

Uncle Vivi sounded deep and more powerful than anyone would expect from such an old man. It made Krenwinkel's gruff voice sound almost angelic in comparison.

We listened to their exchanges – Vivi's deep rumble, followed by Krenwinkel's earnest responses. I could only pick out the odd word from either.

"...strength back…" I heard Krenwinkel say.

"...more…" said Uncle Vivi.

Lizzie looked at me, eyebrows raised.

"More what?" she whispered. "Drugs?"

I shrugged and shushed her.

They talked on.

"...that woman…" said Krenwinkel.

I knew immediately she must have been talking about Mam, and felt the blood rise to my face in anger. Uncle Vivi rumbled a reply, and for a while they didn't speak, but the creaking of the floorboards told us Krenwinkel was moving around the room.

"What's she doing?" I whispered.

"Tidying up?" offered Lizzie, who had started to shiver.

"Tidying what up? You'd best put your jammies on," I said. "I'll get us something to eat in a bit."

"Can I have some…"

"Shhh."

I could hear another exchange from the room above, but

V V

it was short-lived. Krenwinkel's muddy feet appeared once more as she descended the stairs. I quietly closed Lizzie's door and put my ear to the wood, listening to the creak of the steps. There was a pause, and then I heard her again:

"Children should be neither seen nor heard," she rasped. She must have been right behind the door, inches away from my ear, and her words chilled me. "Stay out of my way, or I promise you'll regret it."

And then I heard a curiously familiar noise, that sounded like the rattle of jewellery, a familiar jingle which I couldn't quite place. I waited until I could hear her trudging down the stairs before flicking on the light.

Lizzie looked terrified.

"What was that?" she said. "Has she put a curse on us?"

"She's just trying to frighten us," I said, putting a hand on her shoulder.

"Well, it worked," she replied.

We waited until we heard the front door slam and were certain Krenwinkel had left, before going downstairs to the kitchen. Dirty plates and cups filled the sink, and on the table were half-eaten sandwiches and apple cores. It was as if Mam and Martin had not had the time to eat properly, never mind cleaning up after themselves.

They'd taken their place back on the settee in front of the TV. It seemed to be their usual position now, as if they were on standby before starting their next tasks.

Martin never had a particularly healthy appearance at the best of times, but now he looked even worse. He was ridiculously pale, and his big bug eyes seemed to dart around everywhere in the room, as if he was on the verge of a panic attack.

Mam didn't seem well either. There were dark rings

beneath her eyes, and she had a distant look, as if her mind was somewhere else entirely.

* * *

THE FRIDGE WAS ALMOST EMPTY, and there was no milk, so our meal consisted of dry cereal and a piece of malt loaf each.

Lizzie had grown quiet since Krenwinkel's threat, and I was expecting waterworks at some point. Instead, she got up from the table and walked to the advent calendar that sat on the counter.

"Never mind," she said. "Not long until Christmas."

She opened the cardboard door, cracked through the silver foil beneath, and handed me a piece of chocolate in the shape of a snowman.

"No, it's not long now, is it?," I said, forcing a smile onto my face. "We'll put the decorations up tomorrow, shall we?"

"Yes," she said, smiling apprehensively. "Since Mam is so busy."

Back upstairs, I checked she had everything she needed for school, and then we played a few games of Uno before we went to bed.

I was tired, and quickly fell into a dark sleep, but something woke me in the night.

There were noises.

I could hear slow footsteps and the creak of floorboards.

It didn't take me long to realise they were coming from above. Someone was moving around in the loft room, walking slowly from one side to the other. At times, they seemed to be right above my head, where they seemed to linger before moving off again.

It could easily have been Mam or Martin, but some-thing told me – with no small amount of dread – that it had to be Uncle Vivi.

He was up.

At some point, much later in the night, I fell asleep again and when I opened my eyes, it was light. I was surprised to see Lizzie at the side of my bed.

"I think we're late," she said.

I looked at the clock through gritty eyes. It was 8.30am.

"Yes we are," I said, throwing back the covers. "Go and get some breakfast while I get up, Lizzie."

"But there's nothing there, what should I have?"

"Anything you can find," I said.

Just as we were leaving the house, we passed Mam in the hallway, talking on the phone.

"...no, I'm sorry," she said. "I feel terrible this morning. I'll try my best to get in tomorrow."

I waved her a quick goodbye, and Lizzie tried to reach up to kiss her cheek, but she was far too distracted with the phone call to acknowledge her.

SCHOOL WAS SO BORING.

We were stuck in this kind of limbo, where it was too near Christmas to really concentrate on anything, but too early to give up entirely and start watching movies or playing games. It wasn't just us either. You could tell the teacher's minds were already out of the school gates and buying the first round at the pub.

At breaktime, I was surprised to find Lizzie standing alone by the mobile classroom, looking cold and a little miserable. There was a light fog in the air, which seemed to have bleached the sky and muted the colours of everything else.

"Where's your friends?" I asked.

She shrugged.

"Over there," she said. I looked over at a group of kids hanging out near the wilderness area. "I came to find you."

"Yeah? Are you okay?"

"I'm fine, but I've been thinking," she said.

"That's not a good sign," I said, blowing into my hands to keep them warm, and wishing I'd remembered my gloves. "What about?"

"You know when we were talking about Uncle Vivian? About whether or not he's really our uncle? Why don't we just find out?"

Her nose was running a little, and she wiped it quickly on her sleeve.

"I don't think we should ask Mam anything," I said.

"No, I know she's not well at the minute."

"What then?"

"You know his old suitcase we saw in the loft? Maybe we could… you know, just have a quick look... Find some clues."

I laughed.

"Are you serious? Didn't the last time freak you out enough? What if he wakes up? Or Krenwinkel catches us?"

She rocked on her feet all the time I was talking, desperate to speak.

"No, listen Raine," she said. "I don't think he will. He seems to wake up at night. In fact I think he was up *all* last night," she said. It hadn't just been my imagination – Lizzie had heard him too. "And Krenwinkel comes around seven o'clock. Remember, she said something about the 'agreed time' or something?"

"Yeah, but we managed to wake him last time, didn't we?" I said, feeling a twinge of anxiety just talking about it.

"That's when there were three of us, and one of them was Noah... no offence," she said. "If you made sure Mam and Martin didn't come up, I could sneak into his room, take a quick look and come straight back down."

"I don't know, Lizzie."

"Come on, I know every creak of those stairs, and if we do it straight after school, it'll be ages before either Vivi wakes up or Krenewenkel arrives."

"Let's think about this," I said.

I did too. I thought about it through Maths, Music and double History, all the time with a creeping fear in my belly. By the time we were on the bus home, we had something of a plan. It went like this:

1. If Mam and Martin were upstairs for any reason, or if Krenwinkel was there, then the mission was definitely aborted.
2. My role was that of distraction, which I would do by putting up Christmas decorations, asking endless questions and generally getting in their way.
3. A green for go would be signalled by a quick blast of Christmas music, which I'd Bluetooth to the speaker from the phone in my pocket.
4. Lizzie would then use her well-observed knowledge of the floorboards to climb to the loft undetected.
5. Once in position, she would spend no longer than 30 seconds examining the suitcase and its contents.
6. Danger of any kind would be signalled by a second blast of Christmas music. If this was to

occur, Lizzie was to get back down as quickly as possible.

7. After three minutes, I was to meet Lizzie in her bedroom to confirm her safety, and perform a preliminary review of findings.

We hadn't quite worked out what to do if Uncle Vivian woke up mid-search. I didn't mention it, partly because I didn't want to scare Lizzie, but mainly because I didn't want to scare myself.

When we walked through the door, I could smell freshly-cut timber.

They were busy in the lounge. Mam had her scruffy sweater on again, and seemed to be measuring the window for some reason. Martin was sawing a thin piece of timber, but doing so in a very slow and deliberate way. There were sweat marks on the armpits of his t-shirt, and I couldn't tell if he was keeping the noise down for Vivi's benefit, or if he was just worn out.

He looked ready to drop.

I glanced at Lizzie. She nodded and scampered up the stairs, while I loitered in the lounge doorway.

"Mam," I said. Their heads turned violently towards me. "Er… I was going to put up some of the decorations. If you didn't mind. Just to save you the bother, because I know you're so busy."

Her eyes burned fiercely.

"Alright," she said after a few tense seconds. "But keep out of the way, and no noise."

They went back to work, and I immediately flew upstairs to Lizzie's room. She'd changed from her school uniform into a black top and leggings, so she looked like a little, skinny ninja.

"We're on," I said. "Wait for the signal."

She nodded.

I picked up the box that contained the Christmas tree and carried it carefully downstairs. I weaved my way through Martin's tools and past his suspicious eyes to the corner we reserved for the Christmas tree. I opened the box and started to assemble the tree, keeping watch on them all the time.

I waited until they both looked busy.

Martin had finished cutting the sheet of wood and Mam was helping him to hold it up against the window for size. I pretended to check my phone and sounded the signal. A burst of cheesy Christmas music blasted from the speaker on the sideboard. It lasted only a second or two before I tapped the screen to stop it.

"Raine!" said Mam in a whispered growl.

"Sorry," I said, turning around so I didn't have to see how angry she was.

As the second hand rotated with painful slowness around the clock, I tried to distract myself by putting the tree together. There was a lovely smell coming from the box, which reminded me of Christmas, a combination of wrapping paper, plastic and aftershave. It was as if we'd managed to package a little piece of festive spirit when we'd boxed it up so long ago in January.

The room was eerily silent.

Mam and Martin worked without saying a word or making more than the slightest of noises. The second hand was coming up to its second rotation when I heard a distant noise from above. It was a barely audible knock. Mam was standing on a stepladder, trying to remove a curtain rail, and didn't appear to have noticed it, but Martin's eyes immediately flicked upwards.

He got to his feet and wiped his sweaty brow, eyes fixed to the ceiling. I felt a wave of panic explode and rise from my legs to my stomach, where it sat in a whirl of nausea.

"Martin," I said. His eyes dropped to look at me. "Can you help me with this top bit?"

I made a big show of faking that I couldn't fit the top piece of the tree onto its artificial trunk. He raised a finger into the air, listening intently.

I bit my lip.

Seconds passed, but there was no more noise. He walked towards me, scowling, snatched the piece from my hand and rammed into place.

"Thanks," I said, meekly.

I spent the next few minutes spreading the fake plastic branches and twigs out and trying to make it look even.

"I'll just go and find the lights," I said after a while.

Neither of them replied, so I quietly went off to Lizzie's room, taking the steps two at a time. She was standing in the corner, with her arms crossed, looking a little annoyed.

"Where have you been?" she said.

I have to say, I felt a little proud of her at that moment, and a little bit guilty too.

"What did you see?" I asked.

She handed me her phone and I looked at the screen. The first photo showed the open suitcase, which had a scruffy brown, chequered lining. Inside was a dull bronze war medal.

"That's all there was in there," said Lizzie. "Go to the next one."

I flicked the screen to reveal a closeup of the medal. It was diamond-shaped, with a crown on the top and a wreath, which was crossed in the centre by two swords. A tattered red, white and blue ribbon was attached to a ring at the top, and a banner across the middle read '1914-15'.

"That's World War One," said Lizzie.

"I know," I said.

"Keep going," she urged.

The next photo showed the reverse of the medal. There was an engraving:

6813
P$^{\underline{TE}}$ Virandi

"Looks like that's his real name then," I said.

LIzzie nodded earnestly.

I flicked to the next photo. It showed something on the bare floorboards of the room, but it was too dark to make out. It could have been a slug covered in slime. I sensed Lizzie's breathing grow quicker at my side.

"What's that?"

"Can't you see?" she said.

"It's a blood bag, but it was leaking and when I looked closer, I could see…"

"What?" I said when she paused for too long.

"Teeth marks."

I looked at her, then back at the photo. It was too grainy to make out any level of detail, but I had no reason to disbelieve her.

"That's crazy," I said.

"There's one more," she said.

I flicked the screen with my thumb and saw the luggage label. It was dark and blurred, but readable:

Vivian Virandi
15 Barnard Avenue
Hugheston

"Do you know where that is?" asked Lizzie, eagerly leaning over me.

"Hugheston? Yes," I said. "Well, I think I do. It's not that far from here."

"Can you get there by bus?"

"It would be better by train, I think."

I flicked back to the blood bag and tried to zoom in. There were what looked like spots of blood on the ground.

"Raine?" said Lizzie.

"What?"

"Have you seen Mr Socks recently?"

CHAPTER SIX
JACQUES

We'd gone into the garden and called for Mr Socks, but he hadn't appeared. Usually, if he was nearby, all we'd need to do would be to rattle his water bowl, or kick the cat flap and he'd come running in from the hedge. But it wasn't unusual for him to go missing for a few days either. Once he'd been away for the best part of a week before swaggering in, smelling of old lady's perfume. Mam said he'd just been on his holidays.

We were still outside when Krenwinkel arrived, so we stayed in the garden a little longer just to keep out the way. It occurred to me that a routine was being established. Krenwinkel would appear, bringing with her the usual tensions between her and Mam. Then at night, we'd hear Uncle Vivian shuffling around, doing God knows what.

And it wasn't just the noise. That strange smell we'd noticed in the loft seemed to have pervaded the entire house. It was like the dirt in the fields, the trenches of the Somme, the blood on the floor of a butcher's shop, a thousand musty books left to rot in a second-hand book shop. It reminded me of when we'd all caught tonsilitis and the doctor had given us these strong antibiotics. You could smell it on your breath, and even when you had a wee. It seemed to seep from everyone's pores. But the difference was that the antibiotics eventually made us better. And Uncle Vivian seemed to be making everything worse.

* * *

THE SMELL SEEMED to follow me to school. It was in my clothes and hair. After lunch, I met Lizzie outside the mobile classroom while everyone else played around us. It was cold and there was a gentle drizzle, so she had her hood up, her little face framed by a wreath of white fur.

"Mam didn't go to work again," I said.

"How will Dorothy get up?" she replied.

Dorothy was an old lady who'd been nice to Lizzie once when she'd visited Mam at work. She'd been dead for ages, but no one had the heart to tell Lizzie.

"It's okay," I said. "They'll get some extra help."

"Mam's not even ill," said Lizzie.

"No," I said, although I knew that wasn't true at all – something was very wrong with her.

Lizzie fell silent and absently picked at the rotten wood in the classroom's window frame.

"So are we going to Hugheston?" she said eventually.

I sighed.

"What for?"

"To find out where Uncle Vivi came from."

"I don't care where he came from, I just want him to go back there," I snapped.

"But we might find some clues."

"Clues? What do you mean, Lizzie?" I said. "We can't

just jump on a train and go miles away. What would we tell…"

"What would we tell Mam? She barely even sees us when we're right in front of her, Raine," she said. Her voice had raised slightly and I knew from experience that once her temper got up, it was hard to bring down. "We can tell her whatever we like," she went on. "I really don't think she'd care."

"Yeah, but anyway, how do we get a train to Hugheston when we've got no money?" I said.

"I've got…"

Suddenly, a football flew in between us. It bounced away, leaving a muddy imprint on the wall. Noah came bounding towards us, his hoodie soaked through with the rain.

"What are you losers up to?" he said, grinning.

"Oh, Noah," I said. "Just… get lost, will you?"

He looked crestfallen and I instantly felt bad.

"Sorry," he said. "Are you okay? Has something happened?"

One of the boys behind him shouted his name, but he threw them the ball and waved them away.

"Yeah, we're just having a private conversation," I said.

"No," said Lizzie. "Maybe he can help."

"Help with what?" he said and leaned against the wall between us.

So we told him.

His eyes lit up at the mention of Uncle Vivi and by the time we'd finished, he was already planning the trip.

"I've got the train loads of times and never paid once," he said. "It's a breeze."

He looked at us, raised his eyebrows and gave a grin that seemed to be wider than his face.

* * *

A TRAIN TOILET might not feel particularly small, until there are three of you in there for over an hour.

Straight after school, we'd taken the bus into town and walked through the open barriers at the train station. It took us a minute or two to work out which platform we needed, and found it just as the train rolled in.

Noah's master plan of hiding in the loos was working. He let me have the only seat ('I'm a gentleman', he said), with Lizzie perched on the basin and Noah looming over us both from the corner.

It was a basic bone-rattler rather than one of those plush long-distance trains with tables and sockets to charge your phone. The carriage hadn't been that busy when we'd got on, just a few old shoppers heading home before the rush hour.

"All tickets," we heard the conductor say repeatedly, getting louder as he approached. There was a loud rap on the door. "All tickets please."

Noah held up a hand, which seemed to tell us to be both quiet and to relax.

We waited.

Lizzie's eyes were as wide as frisbees, and she gripped the edge of the basin until her knuckles turned white.

"Right," said Noah. He quietly unlocked the door and eased it open to peek out. "Okay, go."

We followed him as he darted across the aisle into the toilet opposite. As soon as we were all in, he locked the door.

"That's it?" I asked. "That's your plan? Hop from one loo to another?"

"I'm telling you, it works," he said. "The conductor will come back, see that the first toilet's empty and assume he's either caught up with them and punched their ticket, or that they've got off the train. He'll also see that this toilet is occupied and assume someone he's already dealt with is using it."

He tapped his temple with his finger. There was a very simple logic at play that seemed too good to be true. We listened to the announcements until we heard:

We will shortly be arriving at Hugheston.

We waited until the train came to a stop. Noah opened the door and joined a small queue of people waiting to get off.

"Excuse me please," said a voice from behind us. "Can I see your tickets?"

I looked around and saw the conductor, a ruddy-faced man with a V-neck sweater stretched to bursting across his round little belly.

"Noah?" I said.

"Run," he said.

As we pushed our way off, I heard the conductor angrily shout something else, but we were gone. I grabbed Lizzie's hand and ran behind Noah across the platform, dodging the people we found in our way. I looked ahead and saw two platform attendants and a line of stainless steel ticket barriers, where people were tapping their travel cards to get through.

"Noah?" I said again.

"We'll have to jump," he shouted.

One of the attendants saw us as we sprinted towards them.

"Hey," she shouted, but didn't move from her spot.

Noah vaulted the barrier smoothly, slamming down upon it with one hand and swinging his long legs over. I pulled Lizzie in front of me and helped her clamber to the other side.

"Don't stop," I said.

I put a hand on either side of the barrier and jumped over the turnstile.

"The shop," shouted Noah.

We followed him through the doors, into the warmth of the brightly lit mini-market. An old man raised his bushy eyebrows in shock as we ran past him into the snack aisle.

At the back of the shop, another door opened out into the street. Noah burst through it, almost taking it off the hinges in the process. We followed him into the dark street and didn't stop running until we rounded a corner, where we stopped and tried to catch our breath.

"Does anyone want a Jaffa Cake?" said Noah, producing a box from his hoodie pocket.

"Wait, where did you get that?" I asked, willing my heart rate to slow.

He shrugged sheepishly.

* * *

BARNARD AVENUE WAS a terraced street lined with tall sycamore, with roots that had buckled and broken the pavement. The houses were in a gentle arch, separated from the road by gardens of grass and shrubs. The facades were all a dirty white, apart from one in the middle that had black smoke stains emanating from the boarded windows like the elaborate eye makeup.

"Something tells me that's the place?" said Noah.

I nodded.

The rusty metal squeaked loudly as we opened the gate and we walked up the path.

"Mam didn't say anything about a fire," I said. "No one did."

"Maybe when he fell, he dropped a candle or something," said Lizzie.

Noah and I exchanged a glance.

"We could go in and take a look around," he said.

Noah's comfort zone was much wider than mine or Lizzie's combined.

"I don't think we should break in, Noah," I said. "It's, you know, illegal."

"Er… guys, the door is open," he said, and tapped it with his foot. It moved inwards until it jammed against a pile of junk mail and pizza shop flyers.

"We can't just…" I started.

"What exactly are we looking for?" he said.

I shrugged, sighed and looked at Lizzie.

"I don't know," said Lizzie. "I just thought he might still have some family here. Someone who could tell us something about him."

Noah nodded. He turned the corners of his mouth down, as if he was assessing the plausibility of this, when I knew he was just waiting to get inside.

"Hello," he said through the gap in the door and waited. "Shall we just pop in?" He pushed the door so it was wide enough to squeeze inside. "Well, come on then."

We followed him into the hallway. The wallpaper was decades old, torn and peppered with graffiti. There was no carpet and empty bottles lay here and there on the floor. I found the switch, but the light didn't work.

"I don't like this," I said.

"Raine?" said Lizzie and I found her clammy little hand in the darkness.

Noah flicked his lighter and held the flame above his head. We wandered gingerly forwards, Noah at the front, with me holding onto Lizzie, the other hand on the small of his back.

The kitchen had been stripped of anything vaguely valuable. The cabinets were gone, as were the taps, and there were holes in the walls where the copper piping had been ripped out.

"Lizzie, do you smell that?" I said.

She nodded.

It was less intense, but unmistakable – the earthy odour of Uncle Vivian.

"Ow," yelped Noah, making us jump.

The lighter went out and I could hear him blowing on his burned fingertips in the darkness. I felt Lizzie move in close beside me.

"Noah?" I said.

"Just a second," he said. "My fingers are on fire."

I heard him flick the lighter, the sound of the wheel against the flint – once, twice…

On the third attempt, it sparked to life, and in the flickering light, we saw a dark, horribly scarred face staring back at us.

It looked like a weather-beaten crag at midnight.

Lizzie screamed.

Noah's thumb fell off the lighter's button and we were in darkness again.

"Who are you?" bellowed a gruff voice. "What do you want?"

The lighter scratched to life once more, but the light was moving wildly and I realised that the man had grabbed hold of Noah's arm and was shaking him.

"What business do you have?" shouted the man.

Lizzie screamed again.

"Stop, please," I pleaded. "We're here to find out about our uncle."

"Who?"

"Our uncle, Vivian Virandi."

The lighter stopped jerking and he directed Noah's arm towards us, so he could see us better in the light of the flame. In the fluttering haze, I saw his face more clearly – an old black man with a deep wound on one side of his face that crossed over his eye.

He looked at us, not with anger, but with pity.

"Mes pauvres enfants, que devons-nous faire?" he said.

We looked at each other.

"You're going to have to give us that in English mate, because my French is, like, rubbish," said Noah.

* * *

"HERE'S YOUR MILKSHAKE, LOVE," said the café owner, sliding a glass of pink froth in front of Lizzie.

"Thank you," she said, and took an experimental sip, while never taking her eyes from the man.

He was completely bald, save for a halo of white hair around his crown and a chin peppered with silvery stubble that seemed to shimmer under the fluorescent lights. Now I was closer to him, I could see the hideous scar in more detail. He was lucky that whatever had hit him had not taken his eye completely, but the white was pooled with blood nonetheless. He wore a scruffy green overcoat, and slung over his shoulder was a large canvas satchel that he cradled on his lap.

He watched the café owner make her way back to the counter before turning to face us. We were huddled together at one of those tables that had plastic seats attached to it, so you had to sit close to each other whether you liked it or not.

He looked at us in turn, but his eyes settled on mine.

"You call Vivian Virandi your uncle?" he said. He spoke with a heavy French accent, and a bassy tone that seemed to rumble from deep within.

"Yes. At least… that's what my mam told us," I said.

"Wait. Your mother. What is her name?"

"Helen. Helen Russell," I said.

He grunted and rummaged through his bag until he produced a dog-eared notepad. He flicked through its dirty pages, landing on one with a carelessly sketched family tree. Even though the handwriting was terrible, I recognised some of the names.

"Why do you have this?" I said, placing my hand on the open book.

"Because I chase him for two years. Three," he said. He pulled the notebook from beneath my hand and put it back in his bag. He took a napkin from the dispenser and dabbed at his bad eye that was watering badly.

"Are you a detective?" I asked.

He grunted a laugh.

"Non, je suis pas un détective."

"What then?"

"I hunt him."

"Why?"

"You know why. You know what he is."

"What do you mean?"

"You know," he said. "You must admit it, even if it sounds crazy. Say it. Say what he is."

"He's a vampire," I said.

Noah snorted a laugh, but his face straightened pretty quick when he saw my expression. Jacques turned to him.

"Ah, you're not believing?" he asked. "This uncle, he comes from nowhere, yes?"

We nodded.

"And your parents, they do everything he says, oui?"

"They're like zombies," I said. "And he has this horrible woman who says she's his assistant."

"A servant," he said. "Et les autres?"

"Sorry, who?" I said.

"Others. Servants from other times. They follow him like fools, like lost dogs. Still they serve. Beware of them."

"Why has he come here?"

He dropped his head.

"This is my fault," he said. "He has a house in Barcelona, in Paris, in Verona. I chase him, and he runs. He runs to the house where I meet you. I find him and I… I think I kill him," he pounded his chest with a closed fist several times.

"You mean…" Noah hit his own chest.

"Mais oui," said the old man and took a roll of thick canvas from his backpack. He made sure no one was looking and unrolled it. Inside were several sharpened pieces of wood and a heavy-looking mallet. "Through the heart. Not the only way, but a way. And I came this close," he held up a thumb and forefinger and narrowed his good eye. "Now he comes to you."

"Why?" I said.

"He comes to heal. There is power in family," said Jacques. "That is why he comes to you," he said.

"He's… he's horrible."

"You are sisters, yes? Well, there is power in you two also. Be strong together. You can beat him. I will help."

Lizzie, who had been absorbing every word silently, came to the end of her milkshake with a loud slurp.

"What's your name?" she asked.

"Jacques," he said. "I am Jacques."

WE WERE ALL TIRED, and more than a bit unnerved by the events of the afternoon, and we said very little to each other on the train. The carriages were close to empty and because we saw no conductors, we took our chances and sat in the seats. I tapped the mobile number Jacques had given me, scrawled on a napkin from the café, into my phone and hoped I wouldn't need to use it.

By the time Lizzie and I got in, Mam and Martin were asleep in the lounge, TV babbling away to itself..

"Can I sleep with you, Raine?" said Lizzie, looking at me with sleepy eyes on the landing.

"Of course," I said, and we snuggled together in my narrow bed, still in our school clothes. When we heard Vivi moving around upstairs, I felt her arm around me tighten, but in time, her grip loosened, her breath grew deeper and she began to snore gently.

CHAPTER SEVEN

G

something was different.

After school, we came in to find Mam making tea. She'd tidied the kitchen and had something under the grill. She was wearing another smart summer dress – cream with a pink floral print. There was buzzing, something between excitement and hysteria that put me on edge. She hadn't seen me standing in the doorway, and I watched her for a minute, trying to absorb this little piece of semi-normality. I even thought about talking to her, but Lizzie appeared at my side and tugged at my coat.

"What's up?" I said.

I followed her to her room.

"Shut the door, Raine," she said.

I joined her at the window. It was getting dark, and what little light remained was sinking rapidly into the horizon. "Look. Just by the hedge," she pointed. "See?"

It took a while to see them. First I noticed only movement, which could have been the bushes blowing in the breeze, but as my eyes became more accustomed to the semi-darkness, I could make out figures – silhouettes of people lurking outside.

"I think it's *Les Autres*," she said.

"How many?"

"I think there's four," she said.

"They can't see us, can they?"

"Not unless we put the light on," I said, although I wasn't entirely sure.

"They're not going to try and get in, are they?" said Lizzie.

"No I don't think so," I said. "I think if they wanted to come in, they would have done it by now."

"What's stopping them?"

"I don't know. Jacques said they were old servants, so maybe they can't come in because he has new ones," I said.

"Mam and Martin?" I nodded. "And Krenwinkel," I added.

"Does that mean they'll end up like them outside?" she said.

I thought back to that awful dream, the confused and ravaged people, their ragged clothes and desperation.

"I hope not," I said.

* * *

THE FISH FINGERS were cold and the baked beans had congealed, but we ate it nonetheless, happy that Mam had made it for us. Afterwards, she told us to sit with her and Martin in the lounge to watch TV. He was wearing a suit I couldn't even remember him owning. But I could still smell him, the pungent odour of stale sweat. He'd dragged a battered old high-backed armchair into the lounge that had stood in the corner of the dining room for years.

I tried to ignore it.

We watched a Christmas pantomime that had been recorded in a grand old theatre, featuring the presenters of a children's TV channel we used to watch. The camera kept cutting to a crowd of children as they laughed, shouted and pointed at the stage. The contrast between the grumpy adults in our lounge and the carefree joy on the screen felt a bit weird, but after a while we started to enjoy it, and I caught Lizzie smiling at some of the jokes.

The doorbell rang and I looked at the time. Seven o'clock on the dot. Mam and Martin sprung to attention to let Krenwinkel in.

There was much discussion in the hallway and Lizzie craned her neck in a vain attempt to hear what was being said.

"Let's just watch TV, Lizzie," I said to distract her. "Hey, can you remember that guy?" I pointed to the man who was playing the king in the story, who'd just received a custard pie to the face.

"Of course I do," she said. "Mister Crumble."

I heard Krenwinkel enter and the three servants make their way upstairs.

By the time they came back down again, the show had ended and the cast were standing in a line, taking bows while bright yellow credits scrolled up in front of them. Just as the ad break began, the door silently swung open and Krenwinkel entered. She wore a wide smile and makeup that was so thick and garish, she could have been in the pantomime.

Vivian Verandi walked in behind her and seemed to bring in some of the darkness from the hallway with him. He was holding onto her shoulder for support, but he was no longer the shell of a man we'd seen in the loft that day. He still had bandages across his chest, but it wasn't the frame of an old man anymore, there was meat to his bones now, there was muscle.

He looked younger. The deep lines on his face were mere wrinkles now, and his hair was thick, black and lustrous. He walked tall and seemed to fill the room. He settled himself in the armchair and fixed me with his pale blue eyes. Mam and Martin followed him in and stood at either side of the chair, while Krenwinkel knelt on the floor in front of him, looking up at him like an obedient puppy.

He took a long time to speak, and when he did, his delivery was slow and deliberate, as if he had all the time in the world.

"So, you are the children who woke me?" he said, with a voice that boomed and felt as though it came from the walls themselves. "It's nice to meet you at last." He spoke with a strange accent. It was mostly English, but with a smattering of other things too, as if he'd collected them like souvenirs.

I glanced at Mam, expecting her to be angry with us for disobeying *The Rules* and waking him, but her face was fixed in cheesy grin mode.

"Yes," I said, cautiously. "I'm sorry to have woken you. We were just curious."

He smiled, but his eyes felt as though they might drill right through me. His hands moved up and down on the arms of the chair, the fingernails like sharpened dirty ivory. I thought of Jacques' horrible scar.

"And where is the other one?" he said. "The half-breed?"

Again, I instinctively looked at Mam, who wouldn't normally tolerate that kind of talk, especially when it was directed at Noah.

"That one doesn't live here," said Krenwinkel, and she smiled revealing cracks in her makeup and lipstick on her teeth. Vivi looked at her with distaste. He shook his head, as if trying to delete the image.

"Well, thank you children," he said. "Your parents have graciously allowed me to join you until I regain my strength."

"Will you be staying for Christmas?" said Lizzie gently, and I was surprised to hear her speak, knowing how scared she was.

Vivi leaned towards her.

"If you'll have me, little girl," he said, with a patronising and slightly mocking tone. "You have made such an effort, after all." He gestured to the sorry-looking Christmas tree in the corner, which I still hadn't finished decorating. "It reminds me of being young." His lips parted, but I could not tell if he was smiling or gritting his teeth.

"When was that?" I said, terrified to speak myself, but spurred on by Lizzie's boldness. "A hundred years ago?"

"Silence, child," barked Krenwinkel. "Such impudence from such a vile little…"

"Quiet," said Vivi, and then he looked at me. "You have quite a mouth on you," he smiled. "Be warned. I also have quite a mouth."

Krenwinkel obediently turned away from us and settled her loving gaze on him once more. Her tweed skirt had ridden up her chubby legs, revealing a pair of laddered and filthy tights.

He seemed to be repulsed by the sight of her and sighed.

"You know, it's getting far too crowded here. You…" he said, staring at Krenwinkel. "Your services are no longer required."

I heard her shocked intake of breath.

"No," she wailed. "No sir, I beg of you. I have all these

gifts for you." She rose clumsily to her feet and disappeared momentarily to the hall, returning with a tote bag, which she held up to him. "Everything to help you recover, to help you rise."

She tipped the bag and an awful collection of items spilled out. Blood bags with hospital labels, but also dead animals, including a large rat, a rabbit and what could have been part of a fox. Lizzie squealed and lifted her feet off the floor and onto the settee.

"Oh sir," pleaded Krenwinkel. "Please."

Vivi rolled his eyes.

"This is really a quite unnecessary level of drama," he said.

"But you must recover," she said. "You must be accommodated."

"Thank you for your service, woman" he said. "But it is no longer required."

"No," she squealed.

Vivi looked at Martin, and seemed to convey an unspoken message to him, because he removed his jacket and walked silently to the toolbox, which still lay in the corner of the room. He flipped the lid, pulled something out and returned to Vivi's side. I realised what it was, just before he used it. Martin pulled the retractable blade down his wrist and the blood jumped out like a leaping salmon. Vivi pulled the wound to his mouth and hungrily gulped down mouthfuls of blood, his eyes closed in rapture.

"Martin," sobbed Lizzie.

He continued for a full minute while we watched, with Mam's sickly grin adding to the horror. Martin swayed and fell to his knees before Vivi released him. He remained on the floor, holding onto his arm to stem the flow. Vivi delicately wiped blood from the corners of his mouth with a long finger.

"You can go now," he said to Krenwinkel, who renewed her wailing and grabbed onto his leg. He glanced at Mam and a wordless instruction passed between them. She wrapped her arms around Krenwinkel's neck in a brutal headlock that silenced her in an instant, then backed out of the room, dragging the older woman with her.

Moments later, I heard the back door open, followed by the sound of a further struggle and Krenwinkel's loud protests. I heard the door slam, and Mam returned to Vivi's side, breathing heavily as she brushed down her dress.

"There now," he said, smiling. "Just the family."

You're no uncle of mine, I thought.

"Oh, but I am your uncle," he said, as if he was reading my mind. He put his hand on Mam's forearm. "I'm this one's great great uncle, I believe." She looked to the floor, blushing like an embarrassed child receiving praise.

"And we're going to get on so well," he said. "As long as everyone does their bit." He put a hand on Martin's bony shoulder. "And your bit, dear children, is already perfectly clear." He transferred a hand to his lips and closed an imaginary zip. "Can I hear a '*yes, uncle*' please?"

He hit us with his laser-beam eyes.

"Yes, uncle," said Lizzie, in a thin, tremulous voice.

"Yes, uncle," I repeated through gritted teeth.

"Wonderful," he said, tapping the arm of the chair with cheerful finality.

Suddenly the doorbell rang, causing Lizzie and me to jump in our seats. Vivi raised his eyebrows and looked at Mam and then Martin in mock alarm.

"Did someone order food?" he said, laughing at himself.

The silence seemed to last an eternity, until the door-bell sounded again.

"Make yourself useful," said Vivi, looking at me. I got to my feet and as I walked past him, his hand shooting out and to grab my wrist and I saw Mam's eye twitch. "Be sure to invite them in, whoever they are."

In the hallway, the cool air felt refreshingly welcome. I took a deep breath and opened the front door.

It was G.

Martin's friend, Gideon.

He stood in his cargo pants and some kind of hideously bright sci-fi hoodie, his hair a mass of wiry brown hair on top of a cherubic, pockmarked face. He hovered with uncertainty, one expectant trainer on the doorstep.

"Oh hi... er..." he stammered. He could never remember mine or Lizzie's names. "Is Marty in?"

"Yes," I said, but I gave a cutting gesture across my neck that escaped him completely.

"It's just that I've been to the shop a few times and it's always closed, and he's not answered my texts. I've sent him quite a few. I just hoped he hadn't fallen into another dimension or something." He tittered to himself.

"He's fine," I said, then I mouthed the words 'no' and 'go'.

"What?" he said, confused. "What are you saying?"

"G?" shouted Martin from the lounge. "Is that you? Get in here, mate."

I stood to one side, and as he barrelled his way through, I picked up a trail of his pungent, oniony odour. I shut the door, dearly wishing I had been on the other side of it. Once in the lounge, he looked around until he saw his friend.

"Hey Marty. Are you okay?" he said.

"Yeah," said Martin, who had put his jacket back on to hide his bloody wrist and was struggling to stay upright.

"Sorry, bud. I've had the flu. I've been too sick to open up."

"Yes," chimed in Mam, who usually didn't have much time for G. "This is the first time you've been out of bed, isn't it love?"

"Yes," said Martin. "But I'm on the mend now."

All this time, G's attention had been distracted by the curious figure in the chair.

"Sorry," he said. "I should go. You probably haven't had your tea."

"No, we haven't eaten yet," said Vivi. " Just an aperitif."

"Sorry," said Martin. " I should introduce you. This is Helen's uncle, Mr Virandi."

G extended a hand, which Vivi left hanging.

"You haven't been suffering from any colds, or flu-type symptoms yourself, have you Gideon?"

"No… er… how did you know my name was Gid-"

"No problems with hepatitis, jaundice or lymphoma?"

"No, I'm fine. Why are you…"

"HIV?"

"No. Are you a doctor or something?"

"No, Gideon. I'm not a doctor."

"It's just all these questions about…"

"You don't have any drug issues? Intravenous injections?"

I could see a film of sweat on G's forehead.

"This is getting weird. Why are you asking all these questions?"

He looked at Martin, who stared listlessly at the floor.

Without warning, Vivi leapt up from his chair and dived across the room.

I can remember when Mr Socks was a kitten, and we bought a red laser pointer for him. He moved so fast, almost too quick to see, as if he knew where we were going to point the light before we did. Mr Socks never moved as fast as Vivi did at that moment.

G had no time to defend himself.

Vivi caught him in a tight embrace and there was an awful crunching noise, as he bit his neck.

Lizzie ran out the room.

At some point, I must have got to my feet, because I found myself standing only a few feet away from them, watching G's expression turn from that of shock to a kind of sleepy acceptance.

"Stop," I said, weakly. "Please."

As G's strength left him, so did his legs, and Vivi took his full weight in his arms as he continued to feed.

"Martin?" said G, looking at his friend before his eyes closed.

Vivi took a step back and let the body drop.

G lay on his back, with his mouth still open in shock, while Vivi wiped his lips with the back of a talon-like hand and resumed his seat. He breathed heavily.

"I think I may have overindulged," he said, patting his stomach. "Well, it is Christmas."

The dutiful servants sprang into action. Mam gathered G's feet together, while Martin took a roll of plastic sheeting from the collection of building materials at the side of the room and laid it out on the floor.

"Mam?" I said, wiping tears from my cheeks, but she was too busy to hear me. The two of them wrapped the body, rolling his heavy frame into the plastic.

"I think it's time for all good little girls and boys to be in bed, is it not?" said Vivi.

"Yes," said Mam, looking up at me. "I think you should

be heading up, love. I know it's nearly Christmas, but it's still a school night." Her voice was soft and kind, but her eye twitched as if something did not compute within.

I FOUND Lizzie in her bedroom, not crying on her camp bed as I'd expected, but watching *Les Autre* from her window. The back door was open, sending a long column of light into the field.

"There," said Lizzie, pointing.

They huddled in the undergrowth, avoiding the light, but jostling for position at the same time. And amongst them, I saw Krenwinkel's wild eyes, her lipstick smeared down her face like the downturned smile of a clown. For some reason her coat was inside out, so you could see the seams and the label.

Then there were noises from below.

Martin appeared, then Mam, both struggling to carry the body, holding onto the plastic as if it were no more than household rubbish. As they reached the end of the garden, many hands came out to receive it, carrying it off into the darkness of the field.

"What are we going to do?" said Lizzie.

I put my arm around her, but the question hung in the air for interminable seconds.

"We're going to get some help," I said.

CHAPTER EIGHT

HELP

The police had vacated their old Victorian building some years before, and the station was now a tiny street-facing retail unit on the side of the precinct.

The middle-aged cop behind the counter sat beneath a single piece of red tinsel garland and looked a little surprised to see three kids at 8.15 am.

We'd filled Noah in on the bus, and he'd listened with quiet awe and horror. He'd been reluctant to come to the station, but if the man in the blue jumper recognised him from any of his shoplifting escapades, he didn't show it. He put down his book and removed a pair of thick-rimmed tortoiseshell glasses. Then he flipped up the counter hatch and led us down a narrow corridor to a tiny room with no windows.

We spilled it all: Vivi, Mam and Martin, Jacques, Les Autres…

And G. Poor Gideon.

I did most of the talking, but Lizzie chipped in with a

few of the details. Noah mainly chewed his nails and looked uncomfortable.

The policeman took our names, and started taking notes, but after a while, he just stopped and listened. He raised his eyebrows several times and asked a few questions:

How many people would you say are living behind your house?

And this woman was hypnotised too?

How old does that make your uncle?

At the end, he smiled, gave us a crime reference number and said an officer would be in touch as soon as one was available.

"Well, he didn't believe a bloody word of that," said Noah, once we were back outside.

"We couldn't just do nothing, could we?" I said.

A steady procession of cars trundled past, all of them taking people to their very ordinary jobs and school, all oblivious to our situation and I suddenly felt very deflated.

"What do we do now?" said Lizzie.

"I suppose we'd better go to school," said Noah.

* * *

WE GOT through the gates with just enough time to make registration. Noah and I left Lizzie at her locker and crossed the quadrangle to our block. Just as we were about to go inside, he pulled me around the corner beside the boiler room.

"What?" I said. The trip to the police station had left

me feeling drained, and I was in no mood for messing around.

His brow was furrowed and his eyebrows were knitted together. He looked me right in the eye.

"Are you okay?" he asked.

"Yes, I'm alright, Noah," I said. "But thanks."

He took hold of my upper arms, his grip firm, but gentle.

"I just wanted you to know, I'll not let anything happen to you," he said. "I mean… ever."

And then with a swish of our anoraks, he hugged me. My body unconsciously stiffened, but after a while, I hugged him back. When he finally let go, he did so with a kiss to my cheek.

* * *

It was the last day of school before Christmas, and there was a buzz about the place that only made me feel more miserable, and the early 2 pm finish seemed a long way off. It didn't help that the teachers' attitudes had a complete lack of consistency. For example, while I was stuck doing a trigonometry test, another class was allowed to watch a movie on the classroom projector.

At breaktime, poor Lizzie reminded me that she still had one more performance of her Christmas show to do before we broke up.

"For the pensioners," she said.

And it was just after lunch, as their minibus rolled into the car park, that I received a text from Jacques. It arrived during double science, while Mr Swinson was trying to get us enthused about photosynthesis. It was short, and very to the point:

V V

We must meet. Say where.

I managed to text a response without Swinson seeing, and told the others about it as soon as we got out.

* * *

We found him in a dark corner of The Beehive, a flat cap angled over his face to hide as much of his scar as he could. The hardened afternoon drinkers were in the bar, and Jacques was the sole occupant of the lounge. The silver stubble on his chin was a few days longer now, and he looked tired. We dropped our bags by his table, huddled around him and told him about the events of the preceding few days.

"I am sorry for this man," he said, after we told him about G. "This time, I will do the job well."

"We went to the police this morning," I said.

"The police?" he said, and laughed a little. "Bonne chance. They will not believe you. When they arrive at your house, he will turn their minds."

"How does he not do that to you?" said Lizzie, who was slowly deconstructing a beer mat onto the table. "Turn your mind, I mean?"

He shrugged and took the smallest of sips from the glass in front of him, an earthy-coloured liquid that could have been whisky or Cognac.

"I am lucky," he said. "I am strong, but when we fight, I feel him in my mind. I feel him try to take it." He held out his large, calloused hands in front of him, as if they were gripping something.

"So, the others... they're hypnotised too?" I asked.

"No," he said. "Not the same. Once, they were like your parents, and like this woman…"

75

"Krenwinkel," said Lizzie.

"Oui. The line to Virandi is broken, but still they come. They have the need to serve."

"Will they… Do you think they'll come into the house?" said Lizzie, voicing a fear I'd had since that creepy dream.

"Non. Only if they are invited, or if Virandi calls upon them," said Jaques. He took another sip of his drink.

"Je pense… I think he can only hold the minds of a few, not many."

"That's good," I said.

"It is good, but you must be careful children," he looked at Noah and I in turn. "You are not yet man or woman, but almost. Tell me you have not felt him in your mind?"

We shook our heads. I thought about telling how Vivi had seemed to read my thoughts that time, but the moment passed.

"How do we stop it all?" said Lizzie, and we all looked at her. "How do we make things normal again?"

Jacques drained the last of his glass with a shudder.

"We kill him," he said.

I felt Lizzie's fearful look burning into the side of my face.

"Is there no other way?" I said.

"Non," he said.

"Can't we just… I don't know… Tie him up? Take him into the country and…"

"Vraiment?" he leaned forward and I could smell the alcohol on his breath. "He takes whoever he wants. He takes this Gideon. Next time, he takes your mother, like he took my…" He stopped himself. "We must take *him* first."

"How do we do that?" I said, after an uncomfortable few seconds of silence, during which the elderly barmaid appeared. She pushed her glasses onto the bridge of her nose and glanced at us impassively, before walking back to the other side of the bar.

"There are three ways only," said Jacques, once she was gone. "A stake through the heart. This you know. This is where I fail."

"Garlic?" blurted Noah.

"Non," said Jacques, and he gave a short, hollow laugh. "No good."

"Sunlight?" said Noah.

"Oui," said Jacques. "He will die in the light. *Poof.*" He made an exploding gesture with his hands.

"What's the third?" I asked.

He drew a line across his grizzled throat with his finger.

"Décapitation," he said.

Lizzie's face twisted and there were tears in her eyes. I put my arm around her, and she let her head fall against my shoulder.

"Ah, ma cherie," said Jacques. "Do not cry. I will get this done. You will be safe."

He put a hand on her forearm.

"It's just so horrible," she sobbed.

"Yes. Yes it is," he said. "Some things just are. But we are a team, yes?"

She looked at him through her tears and nodded. "Say it to me. We are team," he said.

"We are team," I said, ignoring the bad English.

"All of you," he replied.

"We are team," said Noah.

He looked at Lizzie.

"We are team," she croaked.

"Bien," he said. "Now… this is our plan."

* * *

I DIDN'T EVEN SEE it coming.

The blow struck my cheek hard, and sent me flying to the wall. I let myself sink to the floor and looked up. Mam had been lurking in the shadows of the hallway. She towered over me, eyes blazing, and levelled a finger at my face.

"You," she said. "We've had a visit from the police. A report of a 'violent incident'. Was *that* violent enough for you? I'd hate to disappoint you, Raine Russell."

Lizzie stepped forward to help me up, her eyes still red and fearful from our meeting with Jacques, but Mam blocked her with an arm. "You had better get in line, young lady," she said. "Nothing can get in the way of your uncle's recovery. We must…"

"I know, Mam," I said, getting to my feet. "We must accommodate him. I know."

I was trying to keep my cool, wary of evoking more of her anger. Instead, I gently took hold of the hand that had struck me.

"You're not yourself, Mam. I think you know that."

The corner of her eye twitched and the vein on her forehead bulged ominously, but something I'd said seemed to have hit home.

"You… You just… follow the rules," she stammered. "You've always been so *difficult*."

My cheek throbbed and for a moment, I thought her anger had subsided, that the moment had passed. Suddenly, she threw herself forward, ready to backhand me again, but Lizzie jumped between us.

"Come on, Raine," she said, as cheerfully as she could manage. "I want you to look at this new cat video I saw. You'll love it."

She made it look so natural, whisking me off up the stairs, before Mam had a chance to act. As soon as we got into my room, I climbed into bed, curled into a ball and started to cry. She climbed in behind me and rubbed my forehead with her little hand until I stopped.

"It's not her fault," she said.

"I know," I replied. "She's fighting it. You can see it in her eyes. It was the same the other night, when Vivi grabbed me. She didn't like it, I could tell."

"I hope…" she started.

"What?"

"I hope we can get her back," she said.

I turned to her and saw she was crying too. I wiped a tear from her cheek with my thumb.

"She's still in there, Lizzie. She's still our Mam," I said. "If we do what we need to do, we'll get her back."

"But I don't know if Jaques can…"

Suddenly, the door burst open and slammed against my bookshelf, knocking a few paperbacks to the floor. Mam stood in the doorway, holding two white dresses on hangers which she held up to us momentarily before hooking them over the door handle.

"Put these on," she said. "And get yourself downstairs."

They were matching summer dresses, which she'd bought for us a couple of Easters ago. I could see she'd tried to iron them, but they were horribly creased, and there was a burn mark on one.

"Now," she barked with finality, and she was gone, her rapid footsteps rattling down the stairs.

We wiped our faces and got up from the bed.

My dress was tight, but somehow still fit. Lizzie didn't fare as well. She'd grown so much that the short sleeves dug into her arms and the hemline lay high on her skinny legs.

"This is ridiculous," she mumbled.

"It's *all* ridiculous," I said. "It stops tomorrow."

We took our time going downstairs, reluctant to see what might await us. The lounge was empty, so we made our way down the hallway and pushed open the door. The dining room was bathed in the warm glow of candles, and the table was covered in serving bowls. None of the food seemed to go with anything else – baked beans sat alongside rice pudding, plum tomatoes next to wilted salad leaves. It was an illusion of splendour. I could tell Mam had just emptied random tins from the cupboard, and grabbed whatever leftovers she'd found in the fridge.

Vivi's high-backed armchair had been repositioned from the lounge to the head of the table, although he sat some distance from it, as if to make it clear, he would not be eating, that this farce had nothing to do with him.

He was dressed in grey trousers and a tight black shirt that was unbuttoned well down his chest, so that his bandages were visible. His arms and shoulders looked thicker, and there was definition to his pectorals. There was a sense of strength about him, but more than that, he looked like violence waiting to happen, like a coiled spring ready to be released, a trigger ready to be pulled.

His eyes flicked our way and twinkled in the candlelight.

"Ah, girls," he said, smiling. "Finally, you've joined us. Please take a seat."

We obediently pulled out the chairs from the table and sat down. Mam and Martin were directly opposite, looking pale, waxy and listless. Mam had worn the same dress for days and it was dirty and frayed.

She rested her arms on the table and I noticed one of her wrists was marked – a patch of blue-purple bruising, and at its centre were two raw puncture wounds. Lizzie saw it at the same time, and started to rise, to go to her, but I grabbed her forearm and gripped it until she sat down again. Mam looked at me, her lower lip trembling, with an expression that looked almost apologetic.

"You've got your beautiful mother to thank for this…" he rolled his eyes. "…sumptuous feast." He gestured to the food theatrically and his long claw-like fingernails caught my eye. "Feel free to begin, if your stomach's strong enough. I'll be dining a little later." He looked at Mam expectantly, and she glanced at her watch.

I spooned a small amount of beans onto my plate, and slid the bowl to Lizzie, who followed suit.

Martin lifted some salad leaves shakily with a pair of tongs, and looked at them curiously, before dropping them onto his plate.

It was then I realised there was an empty place at the table.

Vivi seemed to sense my thoughts.

"Yes, we're going to have another guest joining us shortly," he said. "Are they known to be so tardy, Helen?"

"No, uncle," she said.

"I should hope not," he said. "Otherwise, one of these two rascals will have to take their place at the head of the table," he nodded towards the empty seat.

"Please no," she whispered, her voice so tenuous, it sounded like an exhalation.

The doorbell rang.

"Who?" I asked, looking at Mam. "Who is it?"

She made no effort to answer, but rose from the table and left the room.

"It's a surprise, child," said Vivi. "Is that not what Christmas is all about?" He smiled and it was only then that I saw the sharp tips of his canines.

A woman shuffled into the room and I recognised her immediately. It was Mrs Marr, one of Mam's workmates from the care home. With her long neck, hooked nose and inquisitive eyes, I'd always thought she'd looked like a bird of prey, but she had always been friendly whenever we'd visited. She looked tired, and still wore a burgundy cleaning tabard beneath her duffle coat.

"Oh Helen," she said, looking at the candlesticks and table cloth. "This is nice. How are you girls doing? Excited for Christmas?"

Mam glared at us until we nodded stiffly. Mrs Marr lifted a bag-for-life into view and placed it gently on the table.

"I've made you a lamb casserole," she said. "I'm so glad you're back on your feet. You had me quite worried for the past few days. All of the old dears have been asking after you too. Are you sure you're alright? You're still so pale."

Mam stared off into the middle distance, either uncertain what to say, or oblivious to her altogether. Vivi raised his eyebrows, and it was as if he'd sent a mental nudge to Mam to kickstart a reaction.

"Oh… Yes, Vanessa," she said, weakly. "I'm so much better now."

Mrs Marr's look of concern remained.

"That's good. We don't want a poorly mum for Santa coming now do we?" She looked at Vivi and offered a nervous smile. "You must be Helen's uncle," she said. "I do hope you're feeling better now too?"

He smiled, with his head resting in comfortable arrogance on the back of the chair.

"Never better," he said.

"Your uncle, you say Helen? He barely looks old enough to be your cousin, if you don't mind me saying." She laughed, a warm, hearty noise that belied her small frame.

Mam helped Mrs Marr take off her coat, which she hung over the chair at the end of the table. She took a seat.

"Have you been decorating?" she said, looking down.

It was then, with a sickening lurch, that I realised that the floor beneath her was covered in plastic sheeting.

"Yes," said Martin, his voice so thin and croaky, it made me wonder when he had last spoken. "We've been sprucing the place up a bit."

"How nice," she said. The room fell into an awkward silence. "You might want to heat that casserole through a bit, Helen."

"Do I detect a hint of the Emerald Isle in your accent my dear?" said Vivi.

"Why yes," she said. "I'm from a place just west of Cork, but I moved to England when I was a teenager."

"Not that long ago, then?" said Vivi.

She giggled like a girl.

"Long enough, I'm afraid," she said.

"So you have Irish stout running through your veins? Potatoes, cream sherry, coddle and colcannon?"

"I… I suppose so, yes," she said, with a titter.

"Delicious," he said.

"I can't say I've eaten all those things," she said.

"But it's in the blood, dear," said Vivi.

"Yes, I suppose."

In a blur, he leapt up onto the table and bounded on all fours towards her, sending dishes of food crashing to the floor. He flew across the room like a diving swift, his clothes flying out behind him, as if guiding his trajectory. Mrs Marr didn't have time to move, but I saw her expression change – her mouth dropping open in shock – before he was upon her. The force knocked her backwards on her chair and onto the floor.

His lips curled back over his snake-like fangs and he struck.

There was an awful hissing sound and a fine spray of blood arched upwards onto the wall.

Lizzie screamed and ran from the room, and I followed quickly behind. I found her in the corner of her room, with her face pushed against the wall, as if she was trying to get as far as physically possible from him.

"It's okay, Lizzie," I said, putting a hand on her shoulder.

"It's not though, is it?" she said.

I hugged her, but she remained unmoving and rigid. After a while, I left her and went to the window, taking my phone from my pocket. I quickly tapped a text to Noah. Across the fields, where the lights littered the horizon, I watched as one of them blinked off and on again.

"It'll be alright, Lizzie," I said. "I promise."

CHAPTER NINE

OL' LOPPER

N either of us slept, or if we did, it wasn't for more than a few minutes at a time, with Lizzie on the camp bed, and me on the floor. We'd listened to the noises from below – the sound of Mrs Marr being wrapped in plastic, of the back door being opened, and her body being handed over to *Les Autres* others in the field.

As the first signs of light appeared around the blackout blinds, I sat up.

"Now?" she whispered.

"Now," I said. She threw her legs over the side of the camp bed and straightened her hair as best she could. "Are you okay?"

"Yeah," she said.

"Are you sure?"

She nodded.

"Let's get rid of him," she said.

I could see a steely look in her eyes that gave me hope.

"You remember the plan?" I asked.

"Every bit," she said.

It was all I'd thought about too, lying on the hard floor

through the night. I'd tried to picture it, exactly as Jacques had described it, over and over in my mind, but every time, something had gone wrong.

And so, we snuck down the stairs hand in hand.

I slowly and silently opened the front door.

Jacques and Noah stood side by side, the old man a whole head shorter than my friend. In the morning light, his scar looked worse than ever, the eyelid which had been nicked by Vivi's vicious claw looked as if it might split in two over his eyeball. He nodded a greeting and offloaded his backpack from his shoulder onto the ground, crouching to unpack it.

I could tell how scared Noah was by the way he was fidgeting. He jutted out his chin defiantly, the way he did when teachers were telling him off, and I could see his fists through the pockets of his hoodie.

"Where's this thing?" he said.

I stepped out from the doorway and reached behind the wheelie bin.

"Here," I said, handing him the heavy implement I'd hidden there the previous day.

"Christ," he said, holding it up in front of his face.

One side of the blade was straight, but the other was curved and jutted out to a point, like the beak of an eagle. It looked like a particularly brutal medieval weapon, but Martin had used it to take down branches and scrub at the back of the house.

He called it the '*Ol' Lopper*', something which he'd say in a terrible American accent. It was rusty, but he took great pride in keeping it honed with regular visits to the key cutters at the precinct. Noah tested its sharpness, flicking the edge with the tip of his thumb. He looked at me and raised his eyebrows, impressed with the result.

Jacques had fully unrolled his equipment on the ground: a large wooden mallet, and several needle-sharp stakes. The fresh, lighter wood of their tips suggested they'd been perfected only hours previously. A small crucifix had been stitched onto one side of the tattered fabric roll. On the other was an old, over-exposed photograph of a little girl playing a recorder. He remained on his knees, as if in prayer. A breeze passed over us and the first spots of rain fell. Jacques picked up the photograph and tenderly wiped a raindrop from it, as if it was a tear on the girl's cheek.

He put the picture back in place, and removed the mallet and three of the stakes. He dragged his backpack closer, and removed a thick length of rope and a long bungee cord which he handed up to me. He got to his feet and slid two of the stakes into his belt, keeping the third in his hand. He adjusted his beanie hat and picked up the mallet.

"D'accord," he said.

AS WE CLIMBED THE STAIRS – me first, followed by Lizzie, then Jacques and finally, Noah – my mouth was dry and I felt nauseous with fear. On the landing, I pointed to Mam and Martin's room. The door was slightly ajar, but Jacques gently closed it. He beckoned to me, and I edged past him, looping the bungee cord around the handle, just as he'd told me. I tied the ends around the bannister and took the stake that he handed to me, sliding it between the two strands near to the door handle. I rotated the stake until it grew tighter and tighter. When I didn't have the strength to wind it any further, I let go and the stake jammed firmly under the handle. I gave the door an experimental shove, but it didn't budge a millimetre. I looked at Jacques, who nodded his approval.

I took a step towards the loft, but he put his meaty hand on my shoulder and the other on Noah's pulling us all into a little huddle. He looked me right in the eyes before fixing the same gaze on Lizzie and then Noah.

"This is pep talk," he whispered. "Follow the plan. Don't do something stupid. We are team." He looked at each of us in turn. "Oui?"

We all nodded. He gestured to Lizzie, who walked to the stairs and took her first tentative step. We slowly followed her upwards, and although the old timber creaked and groaned, we made it to the top with the minimum of noise.

Vivi lay on the bed.

He was still fully clothed, but his shirt was unbuttoned to his naval. The bandage was gone, and a scar remained on his chest, like a fleshy crater over his sternum. His powerful arms looked set to burst free from his shirt, and the veiny hands that extended from his cuffs were curled in a claw-like fashion, as if ready to strike, even in his sleep. He looked more youthful still, jet-black hair spilled out on the pillow like a dark halo. His skin was deathly pale, but there was a contented look to him, a half-smile across his thin lips, as well as a small amount of Mrs Marr's blood, that had coagulated there to a dark, rusty brown.

Lizzie and I took our positions on either side of the bed. I passed her one end of the rope, wrapping the other tightly around my wrist several times. Lizzie did the same, but I could see she was terrified, taking short, shallow breaths, and her eyes darting between us all in rapid succession.

Noah held Ol' Lopper so tightly, his knuckles had

turned white, and he moved his weight from one foot the other nervously.

Jaques came in close to my side, so near I could smell his stale breath. He brandished the stake so we could all see it, and held up a finger from the same hand.

One…

It was joined by another.

Two…

And a third.

Three.

Lizzie and I dropped to the floor in unison, pulling the rope tight across Vivi's chest.

His eyes flicked open and he hissed like a cat, but Jacques was already upon him, leaping up onto the bed with a speed and agility that belied his age. As Vivi struggled, the bed rattled and bounced. I pulled down upon the rope with all my strength, until the rope was tight around my forearms.

From the other end of the room, I could hear the sounds of Noah trying to prise the boards of the room's window.

"Wake up, demon. It is me. We have unfinished business," shouted Jacques furiously. He aimed the stake over Vivi's chest and raised the mallet high.

The bed shook and the rope dug deep into my wrist. I heard Lizzie yelp in pain.

"Hang on tight, Lizzie," I said. "Don't give up."

"I'm trying," I heard her say, but a cacophony of noise

was building, not only the room, but there were other sounds from below – the angry shouting and furious thuds of Mam and Martin trying to break down their bedroom door.

As Vivi struggled beneath him, Jacques was thrown this way and that, but he finally found his mark and pushed the stake into the vampire's chest. Vivi growled, a deep noise that seemed to rattle the very walls. The old man lifted the mallet once more, but just as he was about to strike, something suddenly knocked Jacques from the bed.

Noah had attacked him.

The Ol' Lopper was buried deep into his neck.

Bright red blood pulsed out onto the rusty blade. It was embedded so surely that Noah struggled to remove it. When he did, Jacques dropped to the floor, clutching at the savage wound.

"Noah, What are you doing?" I screamed.

He stood over me, eyes blank and emotionless.

Noah raised Ol' Lopper above my head, and dropped the rope and held up my hands to defend myself from the incoming blow.

Vivi was released.

In an instant, he leapt several feet from the bed, and grabbed onto the dusty rafters above. He hung there for a brief moment, before descending onto Jacques, sending Noah flying in the process.

A widening circle of blood emanated from Jacques' neck.

Vivi caught my eye and smiled wickedly before lowering his head to feed.

Noah quickly bounced back to his feet and retrieved Ol' Lopper, throwing a few practice swings as he closed in on me. There was a high-pitched scream, and it took me a moment to realise it was coming from me.

Suddenly Mam was in the room, quickly followed by Martin. Her arms were around me, dragging me away from Noah, who tilted his head, confused at this new development. In my peripheral vision, I could see Martin had grabbed Lizzie too. The last thing I saw, before Mam pulled me down the steps, was Jacques' face, his eyes still open.

I knew he was already gone.

The next half a minute was a confusing blur.

We were manhandled back downstairs, where the front door was still wide open.

I hoped someone might have heard our screams.

As we passed through the kitchen, I saw *Les Autre* at the window, drawn closer than they'd ever dared by Vivi's psychic distress signal.

They banged against the pane with their filthy hands, and I saw Krenwinkel amongst them, her face squashed and distorted against the glass.

We were bundled into the garage and Martin eyed us with a look of pure disgust before locking the door behind us. We held each other tightly in the cold darkness, trying to catch our breath.

* * *

Slowly, a small amount of morning light snuck in around the garage door, and in time our eyes grew more accustomed to it.

"He got to Noah," said Lizzie. "Took over his mind."

"I know," I replied, and thought for a moment. "It's because he's older. He's almost, you know, an adult."

We sat in silence for a minute or so.

"Do you think Jacques…"

"He's gone, Lizzie," I said.

She let out a single sob, and I held her tighter.

"I expect Les Autre buried them in the fields, like G and Mrs Marr," she said. "It's so horrible."

My eyes wandered to the square outline of dim light at the other end of the garage.

"Let's just get out of here," I said. "All we need to do is press the button to open the garage door and we can run off down the street. We can knock on someone and get some help."

"That won't work though, will it? Whoever comes to the house will get hypnotised and believe whatever they're told," she said. "And we can't just run off and leave Mam and Martin."

She was right, but I felt responsible for her. I wondered if I'd have the strength to bundle Lizzie down the street against her will, in the same way they had dragged us down from the loft.

"But Lizzie, if we stay, we could all…" My voice tailed off.

"It's down to us, Raine," she said. Her head lifted from my shoulder and I could tell something had caught her attention. "I've got an idea."

CHAPTER TEN

MERRY CHRISTMAS

I f we hadn't found the blade, I don't know what we would have done.

In the semi-darkness of the garage, we'd been forced to navigate Martin's haphazard attitude to storage, but we'd found it, and some other things besides, and so we hatched our plan.

A hopeless, desperate plan, but a plan nonetheless, and it was the only one we had left.

By the time Martin let us out, it had been dark outside for a long time. We'd had more than enough time to get things ready. Not just time to prepare our plan and our weapons, but ourselves.

We'd had time to talk about all the silly little arguments we'd had, and how none of them seemed to matter any more. Looking back, some of them even seemed funny.

We'd had time to decide our priorities. If things went wrong.

We had to try and get Mam out, even if it meant leaving Martin behind. And if we couldn't get Mam out, we had to get ourselves out. Just escape somehow and run.

I found the box of snow globes at the back of the cabinet, among tins of half-used paint and stiff-bristled brushes.

"Just like the ones on your windowsill," said Lizzie.

"Let's give them a shake," I said. "All of them. For luck."

I could sense her confusion, but she did it anyway, and we sat shaking them, until we were sure we'd done the lot.

* * *

AFTER WE'D SLEPT for a while, we started to hear noises from the house. I felt Lizzie draw close to me.

"Merry Christmas," she whispered in my ear.

"What? Is it?"

"I think so," she said. "It's either Christmas morning, or it's still Christmas Eve. I've lost track."

"Me too."

Martin led us, blinking through the harsh fluorescent lights of the kitchen, and into the dining room where he ordered us to sit.

There was no extra seat tonight, so I hoped that meant there were no other guests expected. No hapless Gideons or tragic Mrs Marrs to present themselves for supper, and for that I was grateful.

Also, there was no plastic covering the floor – something I was even more relieved about.

Vivi was in his usual place at the head of the table.

He rested his bare feet casually on the tabletop, but something about his temperament had changed. There was no playful mischievousness in his eyes, and his brow was fixed into a sneer. Perhaps this situation, of being under the same roof with members of his own family had amused him for a while. It had been convenient and necessary, but now, after the attack upon him, all levity was gone.

It felt as if he was done with us.

Mam was asleep, or unconscious, with her head on the table, but the fact that her back rose and fell with her breathing gave me hope.

"I knew the Frenchman would appear before long," said Vivi after a minute or two. "He had tenacity, but he didn't taste as good as his daughter in Le Havre. It's unfortunate that blood doesn't age in the same way wine does. It's quite the opposite in that respect. You know, your mother tastes remarkably good for her age. It makes me wonder what yours would be like, Raine. I really think I'll have left the best till last. And once I've partaken of some good, hardy familial blood, I'll be off on my travels. It'll be nice. In a way, I'll be taking you all with me. Family."

He smiled and looked away.

I tried to make eye contact with Lizzie, to let her know I was ready, but her eyes were fixed on Vivi.

I stood up from my seat, letting the chair fall back onto the floor, and whipped the retractable blade from my sock.

"If you want it so much, come and get it," I said, and sunk the blade into my wrist.

Lizzie winced.

Mam stirred from the table, and looked at me. Her expression changed quickly from exhausted nonchalance to deep worry.

The blood poured in rivulets onto my fingers and began to fall to the floor. A few eerie moments passed when the room was completely silent, save for the *pat, pat, pat* as it dropped onto the carpet.

Vivi raised his eyebrows, and it felt like a victory just to have surprised him. I quickly turned and as I left the room, I saw Mam rise from her seat to help me.

"Sit," barked Vivi.

Mam obeyed.

I didn't look back, and broke into a run, passing through the kitchen and into the far reaches of the garage.

Vivi was right behind me, gliding into the room, as if gravity was no longer a concern. He dropped down, inches in front of me.

"What pathetic ruse is this?" he hissed. "You lure me away from your mother? You think you can save her?" All the while, his eyes were on the blood that seeped from my wrist. From the corner of my eye, I saw Lizzie slink into the room. She closed the door and turned the lock. Vivi glanced at her, then looked at me. "You do, don't you? You'd rather sacrifice yourself than see her come to harm."

He placed his palm over his heart mockingly, then grabbed my arm in a vice-like grip. He brought my wrist to his mouth and began drinking. It felt as though my very life was being drained from my body, and I fell to my knees.

Vivi came with me, crouching on his haunches as he feasted. As I felt myself weaken, he looked at me, mouth full of my blood.

"I see it all, child," he said. "Every plot, every scheme."

"Oh yeah?" I managed.

"Yes," he said, belching blood onto the concrete floor.

"Uncle?" said a tiny voice from across the room.

He slowly turned towards Lizzie.

Over Vivi's shoulder, I could see her, reclining on the sun lounger, the soles of her dirty bare feet and the bicycle inner tube that was stretched tight between them. And in the middle of this makeshift bow was one of the cricket stumps we'd whittled to a needle-sharp point with the blade.

I saw Vivi's torso heave as he grunted a derisive laugh.

"Go on, girl," he sneered, rising to his full height, and tapping his chest, taunting her.

Lizzie pulled back further until the rubber creaked in protest, her face twisted in concentration. She took a deep breath and as she exhaled, she let it fly. The stump streaked through the air like a bolt and hit him with a dull thud.

He fell onto his back, and I could see that Lizzie had miraculously hit her mark, but he'd managed to get a hand in the way to defend himself, and now it was pinned to his chest. It was buried deep, but not deep enough.

He hissed in pain and struggled to extract it.

"Quick," shouted Lizzie.

I grabbed the wrist of his free hand and wrestled it to the floor. I felt dizzy, as if I could pass out at any moment, and I wondered how much blood he'd taken from me. But by leaning all my weight on his arm, I was somehow able to keep it down.

And it was just then that I realised we could do this, we *were* doing this. Yes, we were tired, small and weak, but we could beat him.

Lizzie appeared beside me, standing over us, my little skinny sister looking like a colossus in that moment. She held the cricket bat high over her head.

There were thuds against the door – Mam and Martin, activated by Vivi's psychic distress call no doubt, but I knew how solid it was, and nothing short of an axe could bring it down.

"Do it," I screamed.

Lizzie brought the bat down hard and hit true, pushing the stump closer to its goal.

Vivi released an agonised bark, and dark blood spurted forth from his mouth. He kicked and convulsed on the floor, like a toddler in the throes of a tantrum.

"Again," I shouted.

She raised the bat once more, a look of determination on her face and a sheen of sweat on her brow. But before she could deliver the blow, Vivi twisted and spun, like a crocodile in a death roll.

Lizzie was thrown across the garage like a rag doll and she lay in a motionless heap amongst the junk.

Vivi lashed out.

I took a blow to the chest, winding me and sending me into the garage door which broke my fall with a clatter. There was a sharp pain in my wrist and I fell down heavily. From the floor, I saw him get to his feet. He furiously extracted the stump from his chest and pulled it from his palm. He held it in his hand up to his face, so he could look at me through the wound. Already the flesh seemed to be knitting together, the hole slowly closing like the aperture of a camera.

I tried to get up, but there was no strength left in my legs and they buckled beneath me. I glanced at Lizzie and realised with relief that she was moving again. As Vivi walked towards her, she crawled away from him.

I tried to push myself up, and as I put my hand on the floor, I felt warmth against my skin – daylight creeping in beneath the bottom of the garage door.

I looked up.

The button seemed impossibly high, but I managed to pull myself up against a set of wooden step ladders that leaned against the wall, each rung sending waves of pain through my wrist.

Behind me, Lizzie screamed in pain, horror or both.

I pushed the button, the motor whirled and the door began to rise.

I fell back onto the step ladders, completely exhausted.

A growing band of light stretched across the room, all the way to Vivi, who stood over Lizzie, with his talons ready to fall upon her.

As the light hit his feet, they blackened in an instant and he screamed. They seemed to crumble under his weight, reduced to dust, like the ashes of a burnt-out fire. He tottered on his ankles before collapsing onto the floor, his hands and part of his face falling into the light. They blistered and blackened in an instant.

His screaming intensified, the pitch so loud and piercing, I had to cover my ears. He tried to scurry into the remaining shadows, but the door opened fully and there was no more darkness to be found.

Pieces of him, large and small, came away, crumbling into fine black smoke that quickly dissipated into nothingness. His body seemed to collapse in on itself, and the screams abruptly ceased. All that remained was a low pile of thick dark soot.

"Lizzie?" I walked towards her, leaning against the wall for support. Her face was scratched and bruised, but her eyes wide open. "He's gone, Lizzie."

She looked from me to the black stain on the floor in disbelief, her bottom lip trembling uncontrollably. I fell down to the floor beside her, and for a long while, we held each other.

* * *

IT COULD HAVE BEEN GOING on for a while, but at some point, I became aware of banging on the door, and Mam's voice.

"Raine? Lizzie? What are you doing?"

I got up and turned the key in the lock. A draft blew

through, taking most of the soot out into the street. Mam and Martin stood in the doorway, looking tired and baffled.

"Raine, what's going on?" said Mam. There was no anger in her voice, only weakness, uncertainty and concern. "Have you been having a party? There are people in the garden. My god, Lizzie, what happened to your face?"

They stepped back to let us through. If Mam had no memory of the last few days, Martin must have had an inkling, because he looked to the floor and mumbled "Sorry" several times as we passed.

From the kitchen window, we could see *Les Autres*, all of them wearing masks of confusion, looking at each other and around themselves in utter bewilderment.

Krenwinkel was there.

All the malice had gone from her eyes, and she had the look of a friendly old lady who might have snuck out of her care home for the day.

The gaggle of people parted to let someone through and I saw it was Noah. I unlocked the door and he approached with a furrowed brow.

"I'm sorry," he said. "Raine, I'm so sorry. It was like a dream. A nightmare."

I threw my arms around him.

"I know," I said, "It's okay, I know. It wasn't you."

I felt his stubble against my neck and when he looked up, there were tears in his eyes.

"Raine, please tell me what's happening," said Mam.

"We need to let them in," I said.

I stepped out into the garden and took Mrs Krenwinkel by the arm. She smiled gratefully.

"But why? Who are these people?" said Mam.

"It's Christmas," I said. "And they've nowhere else to go."

"Christmas? It can't be," she said, thoroughly puzzled. "Why can't I remember?"

"It's okay, Mam," I said. "I'll explain, but let's just get them warm. Maybe you could put the kettle on?"

"Right," she said. "Right." And she picked the kettle from its cradle to fill it, happy that there was some semblance of normality to grip to.

* * *

By the time Lizzie and I had led them all in, the lounge was quite full. With their ragged clothes and dirty faces, they could have been war-ravaged refugees. I clicked on the electric fire, and once they'd had some tea and toast, they seemed to relax a little.

"That's a lovely tree you have there," croaked Mrs Krenwinkel. I looked over at the scantily-decorated branches and the solitary gift beneath.

"Thank you," I said and walked over to the socket to turn on the lights. While I was there, I picked up the present and winked at Lizzie. We took it to Mam together and crouched beside her chair.

"Girls," she said. "I'm so confused. I'm sure your presents are somewhere, I just can't seem to remember where."

"It's alright, Mam," said Lizzie. "Just open it."

She carefully unwrapped the jumper and held it in front of her.

"It's beautiful," she said, smiling. "Thank you."

She put an arm around each of us, and pulled us tight.

Just then, I heard a loud jingle that made me jump, and I turned to see a dark shadow fly into the room.

"Mr Socks," yelled Lizzie. She jumped to her feet, scooped him up and brought him over to the chair.

He smelled of old lady's perfume.

I looked at Noah, who stood by the mantlepiece. He seemed tired, but had a smile for me. And as I looked around the room, at this weird blend of complete strangers and the people I loved, I couldn't help but smile too.

Printed in Great Britain
by Amazon